# Emma Chizzit and the Mother Lode Marauder

## Other Walker and Company Titles
## by Mary Bowen Hall

*Emma Chizzit and the Queen Anne Killer*
*Emma Chizzit and the Sacramento Stalker*
*Emma Chizzit and the Napa Nemesis*

# Emma Chizzit and the Mother Lode Marauder

## Mary Bowen Hall

**Walker and Company**
**New York**

First published in the United States of America in 1993
by Walker Publishing Company, Inc.

Published simultaneously in Canada by Thomas Allen & Son
Canada, Limited, Markham, Ontario

Library of Congress Cataloging-in-Publication Data
Hall, Mary Bowen, 1932–
Emma Chizzit and the Mother Lode Marauder / by Mary Bowen Hall.
p.    cm.
ISBN 0-8027-3225-9
1. Chizzit, Emma (Fictitious character)—Fiction.   2. Women detectives—
United States—Fiction. I. Title.
PS3558.A37166E44    1993
813′.54—dc20        93-159
CIP

Printed in the United States of America
2  4  6  8  10  9  7  5  3  1

# Emma Chizzit and the Mother Lode Marauder

$\triangledown$

# 1

"WHO-EEEE!" CRIED THE short, slim woman in the bright red sweater and tan jodhpurs. She clambered out of the antique touring car and stood on the running board, waving her Aussie hat. "Who-eeee!" she shouted again.

I nudged my friend Frannie Edmundson. "That's Trooper Hadley," I said. "The yell's her trademark."

We stood shivering in the early spring chill, having assembled in the parking lot behind the Buckeye City Hall to wait for Mother Lode old-timer Amos Fugaldi's first-ever gold panning demonstration. The City Hall was brand spanking new, standing in splendid isolation on a windswept hill behind the old town of Buckeye.

We'd all turned our backs on poor Amos when we heard the sound of an approaching antique car. The engine made a sedate rumble. In contrast, the gears made a constant whine, a sound I hadn't heard since I was a very little girl and cars like that were still in use. We watched with curiosity as the large open vehicle trundled majestically in our direction and then glided to a stop. It was magnificently restored; the deep blue paint gleamed against the wet darkness of the parking lot's rain-washed pavement.

The car's driver looked to be about my age, somewhere in his sixties, and was a plump, nondescript fellow. But no one paid attention to him. All eyes were on Trooper Hadley.

I'd heard Trooper's trademark yell plenty of times, not in person but in her promotions on television. Her specialty was flamboyant, expensive tours she called "hurrahs"—

helicopter trips to the tops of mountains, camel caravans to archaeological sites, dugout canoe explorations in remote jungles, even excursions in diving bells. Trooper was also known for her environmental activism, and had waged countless campaigns for the preservation of unusual and worthwhile areas. She had a talent for getting media attention; her campaigns were nearly always successful.

"Oh, my," Frannie whispered to me. "Do you suppose Trooper Hadley might be thinking about a gold country hurrah?"

"You could be right, Frannie." Now wouldn't *that* be an interesting complication, I thought.

We'd come to Buckeye because of a request from my old newspapering buddy Adelaide Simpson. Adelaide and I worked together in the way-back-when days. I was a clerk and she the reporter/editor of a small-town paper, the *Rumsey Democrat*. She was worried about her youngest son Jimmy, who'd taken a job last year with the weekly *Buckeye Bugle*.

"Something's wrong, Emma," she'd said. "Jimmy's bothered about a major annexation proposal that's coming up in Buckeye. And there's more . . . something serious troubling him. He won't tell me, but I can sense it."

Adelaide was working at a high-powered job in Washington, D.C., and had to stay with it, so I'd agreed to check on Jimmy. I phoned him and he'd suggested we meet here at the gold panning demonstration. I'd been on the lookout, but so far hadn't spotted him.

"Who-eeee!" Trooper Hadley hollered one more time. She strode from the antique car toward Amos, who seemed as transfixed by her as the rest of us.

Trooper was not beautiful, but unaccountably attractive. She looked to be somewhere in her forties, and despite her slimness was deep chested and square shouldered. Her hair was short—blond and gleaming, unmistakably reflecting her Scandinavian ancestry. But I'd heard she also was part Indian; this seemed to be confirmed by her broad cheekbones and even tan. While she walked with great energy, I noticed an unevenness to her stride—it seemed somehow a part of her charm. A woman of contradictions, I thought—also a great deal of charisma. Nonetheless I resented the way she'd stolen the spotlight from Amos.

"Who-eeee!" Trooper called out yet again, speaking in a group announcement voice. "You've gotta be Amos Fugaldi. Real delighted to meet you. The name's Trooper Hadley." She stuck out her hand. "Shake, pardner."

She was sizing him up, it seemed to me. Well, she had herself a genuine Mother Lode old-timer, and I hoped she had the sense to know it. Amos was wearing plain work boots, faded denim pants and jacket, and a plaid shirt. His only concession to showmanship was a red bandana neckerchief, obviously new.

If he was angry at the interruption, he didn't show it. He quickly transferred the shovel he was holding to his left hand and they shook hands.

"Didn't mean to steal your thunder," Trooper said. She glanced at Amos's metal wheelbarrow, standing nearby, and the barrel of water he'd brought out for his panning demonstration. "Would have shown up earlier, but my friend, here . . ." She gestured with her thumb toward the car. "He had to get out and get under, as the old saying goes."

By now the man who had been driving was standing by the car's running board. The knees of his pants were damp, I noticed, and green with grass stains.

"That there's Hiram Cohen," Trooper hollered. "Take a bow, Hiram."

The man's face colored. He stood uncertainly for a moment, then acknowledged the introduction with a quick nod.

"Do y'all know who I am?" Trooper went on, clearly addressing the crowd rather than Amos. "Who-eeee!" She waved her Aussie hat again. "Trooper Hadley's the name, far-out travel's the game." She flashed her famous grin. "Me and my crew just came off our annual River Boat Ramble. We ended up in Sacramento last weekend. Maybe you saw us on television. The Channel 3 people came out to the Delta King restaurant and did a story about our last-night hoo-ha."

I stared at her with renewed resentment. This *was* supposed to be Amos's show.

Trooper turned back to Amos, still speaking at full volume. "Gonna be fascinated to see your panning demonstration, never saw anybody pan for gold before. Now you just go right ahead; I want to know every little thing about how it's done."

Amos cleared his throat uncertainly and glanced around.

I decided to help him out. "I remember how you were going to start," I called out. "You said, 'Anywhere you want to throw your hat down, I'll take a shovel of dirt within ten paces and show you some color.' "

The offer to dig for gold wherever the audience requested had been taken up just before Trooper arrived. "Dig here!" a boy, not yet a teenager, had shouted. He'd taken off the Giants baseball cap he was wearing and thrown it to the ground, his pleasure in challenging a grown-up obvious.

The boy now stood in a defiant, hands-on-hips pose. "I told him where to take a shovelful full of dirt," he said to Trooper. "See, right here. Right where I'm standing."

"Well, how 'bout that," Trooper exclaimed. "Is that what you're going t'do next, Amos?"

The boy's attention focused on Amos. "I threw my hat down. Show me some gold!"

If that boy were mine, I would have long since had him aside for a talking-to. Where were his parents?

Trooper moved to stand beside the boy and casually put an arm around him. "How 'bout that?" she crooned. "Let's you and me just stand right here and give the man a chance to prove his point." She turned expectantly toward Amos, turning the boy with her. Then she remained absolutely unmoving—I was reminded of the way stage actors stand still and look at another actor when it's time for the audience's attention to switch. I was astounded. First

Trooper had spoiled Amos's act and now she was setting him up for success.

Amos rose to the occasion. "We don't have a creek with water in it right here," he said, "so I'm going to use this wheelbarrow for a pond." He scooped several small buckets of water out of the barrel and into the wheelbarrow, and took a shovelful of dirt from the spot the boy had indicated.

"Now, if you're going to try a little gold panning yourself," he said, "there's something you got to know. You don't want to use your pan the way it comes from the store. If you've seen them, you know those pans are all shiny." He held up his own pan. It was dark and scruffy looking. "You got to get them to look like this, get all the grease out. You burn it out."

He glanced around at the audience. The boy stared back at him, captivated.

"That's right, son," Amos went on. "And right now we're going to make sure about this pan of mine. We're going to put in some shredded newspaper, and light a fire."

I imagined the visions of condoned arson that danced in the boy's head.

Amos took out a box of wooden matches and handed it to the boy. "Any oil or grease is going to coat those little tiny flakes of gold, float them out of the pan—that's right, sonny, you just go ahead and set that newspaper on fire."

The flames flared up briefly, struggling for survival in the chilly breeze.

"Fact is," Amos went on, "in the gold mining days, if the folks in a camp didn't like a man, he might wake up some morning to find fish oil in his sluice box. He'd have to throw everything out and start over from scratch, build a new sluice. Or if he was smart . . ." Amos took time out to pick up his gold pan and blow away the last of the flames and charred newspaper. "That's fine," he said. "Thank you, sonny. Now, as I was about to say, the miner who discovered fish oil in his equipment, if he was smart, cleared out of town and set up in business somewhere else."

Amos had his audience locked in tight now. I breathed a sigh of relief. The man knew his gold mining through and through, but he was an amateur where audience reaction was concerned. Earlier, he'd alternately intrigued and bored those few of us who'd shown up early. He'd reached a low point as we'd waded across a little stream through the wet grass on the rolling hillsides beyond the city park. He'd tried to point out traces of long-ago mining activity, but it was windy in the open fields; we caught only about half of what he said. And we had trouble discerning the mounds and trenches he'd told us about because of the lush growth of springtime grass. It seemed to me he should have held off on the landscape tour until the grass dried out and flattened, became a golden carpet that would reveal every bump and indentation.

Amos scooped mud from the wheelbarrow into his pan and began the process of swirling and shaking it, explaining that he would winnow the contents of the pan down to the dark sand—pay dirt. As he worked he talked about the long-ago depression days, when unemployed men flocked to the Mother Lode to try their luck at panning.

My attention was caught by a battered Volkswagen bug just arriving. The driver got out and hurried to join Amos's audience. He was a serious-looking young man wearing glasses with Coke-bottle lenses and a camel sports jacket, much worn, with leather patches at the elbows. The top of a spiral-bound notebook stuck up out of one jacket pocket and a camera was slung around his neck. This had to be Adelaide's son, Jimmy. He couldn't have made his identity any plainer if he'd sent up a rocket.

I nudged Frannie. "There's our young man," I whispered. "I'm going to go over and introduce myself."

"I'll go with you," Frannie said.

The two of us made our way around the back of the group to where Jimmy stood. I tapped him on the shoulder.

"Hello," I said, keeping my voice low so as not to detract from Amos's presentation. "I'm Emma Chizzit."

"I was beginning to think you hadn't made it," he said.

"Mom said to look for a truck that had a sign on the door with your name and 'A-1 Salvage.' "

"My friend Frannie wanted to see the panning demonstration, too. We came in her car."

I introduced Frannie.

Jimmy was very much his mother's son. He had the same light brown hair and it tended to fall across his forehead in the same way. The planes of his cheeks were also the same. And, I thought fondly, his smile was identical to his mom's.

Jimmy apologized for not having been there earlier. "I was taking care of the baby while my wife went to the supermarket." He smiled shyly. "She's pregnant again. I try to make things easier for her."

We agreed to postpone further conversation until after Amos had finished his presentation.

"In any event," Jimmy added, "I've got to move in closer and snap some pictures for the *Bugle* while Amos is still doing things with that gold pan."

While Jimmy was getting his pictures, a car and a pickup truck pulled into the parking lot.

A dapper-looking man with silver hair—a salesman type, Willy Loman style—got out of the car, a late-model Toyota. He then went around to the other side to open the door for his passenger. She seemed younger than he and, though attractive, was no spring chicken. She wore a carefully arranged orchestration of pastels and pearls. I thought it was a bit much.

A man in scuffed cowboys boots, a ten-gallon hat, and too-tight jeans emerged from the truck. He wore a western-style shirt, and a belt with a big buckle. He had one of those top-heavy builds; his belly strained the shirt buttons and overhung his belt. There was a sign on the truck door, "Wemmer's Autos and Trucks. Buckeye's Best Buys." Wemmer himself, no doubt. He walked with a large-frog-in-a-small-pond swagger to join the silver-haired man and Mrs. pastels-and-pearls.

When Jimmy came back from taking pictures of Amos I asked him about the three newcomers.

"The fat guy's Bill Wemmer," Jimmy whispered, "president of the Buckeye Chamber of Commerce. And the couple are Doc Truesdale and his wife—he's the local chiropractor, retired now. Truesdale is Wemmer's partner in a big real estate deal, along with Jonathan McCready, our city manager." Jimmy winked. "Buckeye's elite." He was silent for a moment. "I can see why Wemmer's here," he added, "but I don't know about Truesdale." He allowed himself a wry smile. "Usually the Buckeye glitterati ignore Fugaldi and his talk about the old mining sites here. But the mining sites are included in the land they want to develop." He winked at me, conspirator-style. "Maybe they're getting nervous that too many people are going to start paying attention to Amos."

"Heavens!" Frannie said. "You'd think they'd want to play up the town's history, mining and all that. It ought to be very good for bringing in the tourist trade."

"You'd think so," Jimmy said. "But you're not one of the locals. They don't want anyone getting in their way. Amos's mining sites will be paved flat by the development they plan."

Another car had pulled into the parking lot, a Volvo station wagon that appeared to have a lot of miles on it. There was a magnetic sign on the door: "Barker's Custom Photography."

"That's my friend Howie," Jimmy said. "He's come up from Stockton to take publicity pictures for Trooper Hadley after the demonstration is over." He excused himself, hurried to the station wagon, and began to help his friend unload camera equipment.

"Oooh!" Frannie exclaimed. "Did you hear? Jimmy and his friend knew Trooper Hadley was coming here today."

Adelaide had been right in smelling trouble, I thought. Jimmy was likely an idealistic crusader, just as his mother had been. If he was going to champion Amos against the town's powers-that-be, his job as newspaper editor might be at stake.

Amos had been busy with his gold pan, from time to time

washing muddy water over the edge while he continued to talk about the town's history. Now he announced he was down to pay dirt. It was time to pick out the flakes of gold from his pan.

"Here, sonny, you hold this," he said, handing the boy a small glass vial. "There's just water in there, but once we put that gold in you'll be able to swirl it around and admire how those flakes shine."

The crowd edged forward.

"Look in the pan. You can see the color—those gleaming flakes—in the dark sand." He produced the box of wooden matches again. "Now, sonny, you're going to use the plain end of a matchstick to pick out your gold. That's right, the flat end. Put it down on your flake of gold. Good for you! Now drag it to the edge of the sand, take it out, and put it in your vial."

The boy did as he was told. "I got one!" he shouted.

There was a stirring among the audience and a craning of necks, then a scattered round of applause as the boy held the vial up to the light.

Amos helped him finish collecting the gold flakes, and then presented him with the little vial. "You keep it, sonny," he said.

The panning demonstration had come to a slam-bang conclusion. Even Wemmer and the Truesdales had seemed interested; they'd edged forward along with the rest of us, craning their necks to see. The boy's delight was obvious. The audience applauded again. "Who-eeee!" Trooper yelled over and over, clapping for all she was worth.

Soon after, I noticed Trooper and Mrs. Truesdale exchange odd glances, as if they were trying to determine whether they'd seen each other before. It was only a moment—Mrs. Truesdale turned away and Trooper moved through the crowd to join Jimmy and his photographer friend.

Wemmer, apparently displeased to see Jimmy in conference with Trooper, walked toward them, scowling. He gave Trooper a curt nod of recognition in a manner that suggested he'd already met her and hadn't enjoyed the experience, then put a hand on Jimmy's shoulder and steered him away from the group.

I nudged Frannie. "Look at that," I said.

Wemmer had backed Jimmy up against the tailgate of the pickup and was lecturing him—gesticulating, leaning close. He was angry and impatient, but at the same time I had the impression of someone dealing with a not-very-bright child. Jimmy, his face closed, kept his gaze on the ground. I knew that expression. He was his mother all over again, only younger, more vulnerable. My heart ached for him.

$\triangledown$

# 2

"Hoo, boy!" I said to Frannie. "Adelaide was right. We've got a peck of trouble."

She gazed at me inquiringly. "Take a look at that." I indicated Wemmer and Jimmy.

"I'll bet a dollar to a doughnut that the president of Buckeye's chamber of commerce is bawling out our young newspaper editor for collusion with the enemy."

"Collusion with the enemy?" Frannie blinked. She always blinks when she's confused. "I don't understand. Why wouldn't the Buckeye Chamber of Commerce man want Trooper to bring one of her tours here?"

"Don't forget, Frannie, Trooper is known for protecting resources—including historic sites. And Jimmy told us Wemmer is in partnership with some of the other local folk in an annexation deal that includes the old mining sites."

Frannie blinked again. Then her expression changed. "Oh," she said softly. "Oh, dear."

"Yep. Maybe Wemmer thinks he and his partners are headed for a shoot-out—Trooper Hadley at the O. K. Corral."

"Oh, for heaven's sake, you don't think—"

"I'm not sure what to think yet, Frannie."

I was still watching Wemmer, who by now had finished with Jimmy and was standing off to one side with the Truesdales, deep in conversation with the silver-haired chiropractor. Mrs. Truesdale, I noticed, was still glancing from time to time at Trooper. And she was being sneaky about it.

"Frannie, we're not going to learn anything just standing

here." I grinned, and offered her my arm. "What say we mosey over closer to the action and have a listen?"

Frannie always loves a bit of intrigue. She giggled, twining her plump arm around mine. "Let's *sashay!*"

Our sashaying led past the antique auto where the driver sat on the running board with an air of dejected patience. Frannie's hostess instincts, as always, came to the fore—she can't bear to see anyone neglected. "Hello there, Mr. Cohen," she called cheerily, and headed us toward him.

I reluctantly accompanied her. Cohen greeted us with a wan smile, and we introduced ourselves.

"That's just an absolutely gorgeous automobile," Frannie cooed.

Cohen, who had risen courteously to his feet, was transformed. His shoulders squared; his eyes, behind rimless glasses, sparkled. "Isn't she a beauty? I restored her myself. She's a Lincoln, the L-Series seven-passenger Phaeton."

"Oh! Just think—a Phaeton!"

I was still watching Wemmer and Truesdale. Their air was secretive, almost furtive, and they glanced repeatedly at Jimmy and his photographer friend. Mrs. Truesdale, who stood off to one side, looked here and there with an elaborately casual air. I decided it didn't matter that we'd gotten sidetracked with Cohen and his antique car. We'd have had our work cut out for us trying to do any eavesdropping.

Frannie was still being nice. "Mr. Cohen, what year is your car?"

"Call me Hiram, everybody does. The car's a '26 model. And she's a police special, too. I was really lucky to find her."

"A police special?" Frannie asked in her I'm-*so*-impressed voice.

"Yes, siree! Those police specials were the babies to have back in the twenties. They had trimmings not available to the general public. Lots of V-8 power, and four-wheel brakes. Of course, the police weren't the only ones who had them. Gangsters and bootleggers did, too."

"Gracious!"

Wemmer and Truesdale stopped their conversation momentarily, both turning toward the City Hall building; I looked in the same direction. An older man in a dark gray business suit emerged from the rear exit, having let himself out with a nonchalance that suggested everyday familiarity. He headed toward Wemmer and Truesdale. He had to be Jonathan McCready, Buckeye's city manager and the third partner in the real estate deal.

I studied McCready, wondering what he had in common with the other two investors aside from their business venture. Not much, I concluded. His dark suit and tie were conservative, even slightly out of date, but decidedly first-class. He wore a white shirt and, I was willing to bet, cufflinks. Furthermore, he had an air of authority about him, a bred-in-the-bone confidence.

By now Hiram had opened the front door of the car. "See," he said to Frannie, "I had the upholstery made of the original type of leather—just run your hand over that—the pattern and stitching are the same as when the car was new."

I had a look, too, and was impressed with Hiram's thoroughgoing sense of detail.

"Just look at this," Hiram said, indicating the dashboard. "The instruments are rebuilt; they're all like the originals."

"How impressive," Frannie said. "And the car's so shiny and pretty, just like new. That's a gorgeous color."

"Cobalt blue." Hiram's voice vibrated with pride. "One of the three original colors."

He closed the door, and then opened the hood and began pointing out various features of the engine to Frannie. I'm sure she understood not a word he said, but she gave forth a plentiful supply of *ooohs* and *ahs*.

I hoped that Jimmy would fill me in later on the particulars of his dispute with Wemmer and company, and turned my attention to Cohen's automobile.

I'm always interested in old-time items—where people get them, how they restore them, and, above all, how you find out how much things are worth and how to go about selling them. I have a part-time business, A-1 Salvage. I clear out old houses and buildings, contracting to do the work for a set amount, plus the right to sell anything of value I find. A lot of people think it's an odd business for an older woman, but it suits me. I live rent-free in the old chauffeur's apartment above Frannie's garage and do odd jobs for her. With what I make from my business, plus a little bit of Social Security, I can stay afloat financially.

"Where did you find this car?" I asked.

Hiram launched into a long explanation, beginning with his good luck at finding the remains of the old Lincoln rotting away in a barn in the southern Mother Lode, near Sonora. As he talked, I kept watch not only on McCready, Wemmer, and Truesdale but also on Trooper, Jimmy, and the photographer, who by now had been joined by Amos Fugaldi. Trooper's Operation Photo Opportunity was about to commence. Barker had collected his cameras and equipment; the group headed out across the wet green field behind the city hall.

I interrupted Hiram. "I'd like to hear the rest of your story, but maybe later. I want to watch the picture taking."

He was obviously disappointed, but with good grace accompanied Frannie and me toward the field.

At this point, Wemmer, Truesdale, and McCready concluded their conference with a round of nodding—apparently they'd reached agreement on something. Wemmer strutted back to his truck. Truesdale gallantly held open the door of the Toyota for his wife. McCready headed toward an older-model Chrysler parked at the rear of City Hall.

Trooper, waiting while Jimmy and the photographer had Fugaldi try out various poses with his gold pan, was the first to spot us coming. "Who-eeee!" she called. "Hiram, bring your friends right on over and we'll all get acquainted."

"I'm Emma Chizzit," I said, "and this is my friend Frannie Edmundson."

"It's just grand to meet you. You folks from Buckeye?"

"No," I told her. "We came out from Sacramento to see the panning demonstration, just like you did."

"And Jimmy Simpson asked us to stay," Frannie added. "Emma knows his mother."

"So you already know Jimmy. Now isn't that just grand. You know our photographer, too? A friend of Jimmy's, Howie Barker."

Barker, busy unfolding a portable reflector, acknowledged the introduction with a brief nod.

I tried to place Trooper's accent. She had less of a drawl than a twang. Missouri or Colorado, maybe, definitely not Old South.

"Now, Amos, do you know these folks?"

Fugaldi straightened and turned from where he'd been testing the creek dirt with his shovel. Trooper introduced us.

Howie, the photographer, took over then, with a lot of fussing about how Amos and Trooper should pose with the gold pan. Jimmy was assigned to manage the reflector, and there was more to-do about getting just the right light on Amos's and Trooper's faces.

There was nothing for Hiram, Frannie, and me to do but play the role of spectators.

"Have you known Trooper long?" I asked Hiram as I watched Barker maneuver Amos and Trooper into a new pose.

Hiram blushed. "No. Just since the River Boat Ramble. Actually, not really until it was over."

"Oh? How's that?"

"Well, there were maybe forty of us on the tour. I hardly had a chance to get acquainted with Trooper."

"Um hum," I said, still watching the photo session.

"Of course," Hiram went on, "I had a few conversations with Trooper. She gets around to talk to everybody who comes on her hurrahs, you know. I told her about the car, how I restored it and all."

Undoubtedly.

"And the other day—Thursday, I guess—she called me up, out of the blue. She wanted to know if I could meet her in Sacramento and bring her out here."

"To take pictures?"

"Yes, siree! And as soon as they finish with the gold panning shots, the photographer's going to take pictures of her and me and the car."

So Trooper had been planning the visit this Sunday at least since Thursday. Earlier, probably—she must already have made the decision to come to Buckeye and get photographs.

Hiram and I watched in silence until the picture-taking was finished.

"Now, don't y'all go away," Trooper said. "We've got a couple more pictures to take here, and then we're all going to have champagne and caviar, courtesy of Trooper Hadley."

"Gracious!" Frannie said, obviously pleased with Trooper's sense of occasion.

Howie posed Trooper and Hiram by the old Lincoln, taking a lot of time and care. When the photo session at Hiram's car was ended, Jimmy got out his own camera and invited us to pose with Amos and his gold pan, the new City Hall in the background. Then he posed us with Trooper by Hiram's car, also with City Hall in the background.

"These shots are for the *Buckeye Bugle*," he told us. "The folks around here think City Hall is the center of the universe."

"Who-eeee!" Trooper hollered. "It's champagne and caviar time! Hiram, honey, why don't y'all go over to the car and fetch the fixings?"

I glanced around, wondering how our picnic was going to work out. The new city hall with its freshly paved parking lot had no landscaping or other amenities. And it was unpleasantly windy.

"This isn't a good place for a picnic," Amos said. "Why don't you let me lead you over to the old Nye District School? It's down a ways from here, just across the railroad tracks. The school's abandoned, but we can use the old gazebo in the yard."

"That's a fine idea," Trooper exclaimed. "Lead on, Amos!"

We made quite a procession. Amos first, in an old pickup that was even more battered than mine, and then Trooper and Hiram in his antique car, Frannie and me in her Mercedes, and Jimmy and Howie in their cars. We proceeded down the windswept hillside and turned west when we got to Route 18, the highway leading from Buckeye down toward the Sacramento Valley. Highway 18 dips down into a hollow, where we crossed some railroad tracks and, beyond, turned off into the old schoolyard.

The schoolhouse looked forlorn. But, as Amos promised, in the yard was a gazebo. It sheltered a picnic table.

"Isn't this just *grand!*" Trooper exclaimed as soon as we'd all piled out of our cars. She turned to the photographer. "Now, Howie, would you get out that camera of yours again. I'd just love to have a couple a pictures of Amos and me and this here schoolhouse."

I volunteered to help Hiram unload the picnic fixings, figuring it was my best chance to learn about the business aspects of restoring old cars.

"How did you go about finding the things you needed to restore the Lincoln?" I asked as he pulled a heavy cold box from the back seat.

"Well, you got to have a lot of luck. For instance, for the artillery wheels—that's what you call wheels with wooden spokes—I located a specialist through *Hemming's Motor News.*"

"*Hemming's Motor News.*" I repeated the name out loud to be sure I remembered it. I keep a mental file of publications I can look up in the library.

"Trooper's got the champagne and caviar in this cold case here," Hiram said to me, "and the glasses and plates and that sort of thing in that wicker hamper."

"I can take the hamper," I said.

I thought I heard an odd sound as I pulled it off the backseat, but my mind was still on reference sources for old cars and their appurtenances; I didn't really pay attention. But when I started walking with the hamper, I heard the sound again, and, belatedly, recognized it for what it was.

I nearly dropped it. Instead, I took a deep breath, set it down gently, and double-checked to see that the lid was securely latched.

"Hiram," I said. "We've got a problem with this hamper. There's a rattlesnake in here."

$\triangledown$

# 3

T HERE'S NOTHING LIKE a rattlesnake for creating a hulla-
baloo.

Amos immediately went for his shovel. Howie and Jimmy
scrambled to get out their cameras. "This will make a great
spot news photo," Howie exclaimed.

Trooper went into crowd control mode and tried to keep
us all calm and shooed back a safe distance. I was grateful
for Frannie, inasmuch as she made a wonderful crowd person. She held back, frightened, emitting "Oh, dear!" and
"Gracious!" exclamations. I searched for something useful
to do, knowing full well that Amos must be experienced at
dealing with snakes. I stood beside Frannie, offering reassur-
ances. And Hiram at last roused himself to action, hurrying
toward his Lincoln. "I've got a portable phone in my car. I'll
call the sheriff."

Amos approached the picnic hamper with an air of calm
expertise. He unfastened the latches and stepped back, then,
with a flourish, used the blade of his shovel to flip up the lid.

We waited.

"He'll be moving slow," Amos said. "It's pretty cool for a
snake to be out and about."

"Wait!" Howie yelled from where he was rummaging in
the back of his station wagon. "Wait! I have to change the
lens on my camera."

The rattler emerged from the hamper, its sleek sides
gleaming in the spring sunlight. It was big, more than three
feet long, and thick as my wrist around the middle. Its tri-

angle-shaped head moved from side to side, questing.

Amos struck as soon as the snake's head was on solid ground, decapitating the creature with one solid thrust. He held the shovel blade in place while the body thrashed with astonishing violence. It was all over in a few seconds. I suddenly felt sorry for the snake.

Frannie was the first to creep forward for a close look. "Oooh," she said, and shuddered. Then she crept closer, making a transition from fright to fascinated revulsion. "Yech!" she said. "I didn't know snakes *bled*."

"Damn!" Howie said to Amos. "Why didn't you wait until I had my camera out before you killed it?"

Amos looked at him gravely. "I wasn't thinking about pictures."

I regarded the snake's contorted body, and the severed head. "I'm just as glad you weren't," I said.

Howie got down for a close look at the dead rattler. "Damn! This would have made a great news photo." He fiddled for a minute with the camera, which hung around his neck, taking off and then replacing the lens cap. "I might have gotten big bucks for a shot of the snake thrashing around like that."

Jimmy stepped forward with his camera. "For the *Bugle*, it doesn't have to be wiggling." He snapped several pictures. "Of course," he added, with what I thought was a touch of resentment, "I don't get paid any extra for doing the photo work, either."

Hiram came back from his phone conversation with the Tengold County Sheriff's Department. "They've dispatched men," he said, "but it'll be twenty minutes before they're here. We're not supposed to touch anything until then."

"Who-eeee," Trooper said softly. She nudged Amos in the arm. "I hate to see any wild creature killed, but I'm mighty glad you took care of that snake before we got our instructions from the sheriff's department."

Everybody laughed nervously. Then we all settled into waiting for the deputies to arrive.

We didn't talk; even Trooper was quiet. There seemed to be nothing to say, except to speculate about who had put the snake in the hamper or which one of us it was supposed to have bitten. Not cheery conversational material, that.

I sat in the schoolyard's old gazebo, thinking of all the tales I'd heard about old-timers' tricks with rattlesnakes—macho stuff. Just funning. I'd never thought fooling around with poisonous snakes was a sane idea, let alone *fun*. But someone had used an old-time prank to discourage Trooper. Or maybe even Amos. Or, for that matter, the message could have been directed at Jimmy—a warning to keep his activities in line with what the Buckeye powers-that-be wanted.

No, Trooper had to be the target. She was the one with the reputation for saving the environment. And she was the one with the lightning rod personality—witness my own feelings about her. She was charismatic, a fascinating person, and at the same time downright annoying. She was the lightning rod, and trouble had struck.

Spur-of-the-moment trouble. No one could have known that Trooper would bring the picnic hamper. Also, she'd only announced her champagne party at the last minute.

The sheriff's men arrived: two deputies. They so strongly resembled each other they could have been a father-and-son team. Both wore aviator-style dark glasses. Both had full mustaches—one dark brown, the other salt-and-pepper.

"We have to consider this attempted murder," the older of the two told us. "Attempted murder," he repeated solemnly, as if quoting from a rule book, "an attempt on the life of one or more of the parties involved."

"We put in a request for a definition of the crime while we were driving out here," the younger one said.

By the rule book, sure enough. I studied the deputies' expressions. They wore poker faces, both of them. There was no telling whether they were actually taking this as seriously as the rules said they should.

Our attention was diverted by the sound of a police siren. A black-and-white patrol car, lights flashing, came down the hill from Buckeye and pulled into the schoolyard. The emblem on the door identified it as a city of Buckeye vehicle.

"The sheriff's department calls must have been monitored on the Buckeye police radio," Jimmy said. "Now we're really going to get official."

The policeman who emerged from the vehicle was incredibly heavy, muscular as well as fat. The car rocked when released from his weight.

"Officer Francis O'Rourke," Jimmy announced, sotto voce. "Otherwise known as Palooka."

The policeman waddled to where the two deputies stood. The man was enormous, and every inch a palooka. His skin was scarred, as if from acne, and his nose looked as if it had been through a hundred prizefights. He stood stolidly, listening to the two sheriff's men explain the situation, nodding with his mouth held slightly open, glancing from time to time at our little group.

"This is Buckeye's finest?" I asked Jimmy.

"We have three men on the force," Jimmy said. "But Palooka puts in more time than any of the others. His main claim to fame is that he's good at keeping order at high school football games. He's also pretty good at keeping the local doughnut shop in business."

I could well imagine.

Another car pulled into the schoolyard. It was McCready. He parked his Chrysler beside the Buckeye police car, got nimbly out, and, with a nod in our direction, went to join the deputies and Palooka.

Their conversation was brief. Palooka returned to his car, inserted his ponderous weight into it, and left. McCready shook hands with the two deputies, then came over to speak with our group. He still wore the gray business suit. And cufflinks—I'd been right about that. His thinning hair, neatly combed back, was a colorless shade, somewhere between brown and gray. I couldn't peg his age. He might have been sixty or more.

He nodded a greeting to Jimmy and Amos, and shook

hands with the rest of us. "Jonathan McCready, Buckeye city manager," he repeated each time, listening to our names with an air of careful attentiveness. Nevertheless, under the smooth exterior, he was nervous. The muscles in his jaw pulsed with a recurrent tic; he held his body rigid.

"Everything is going to be just fine," he assured us after the introductions were complete. "The sheriff's boys are about finished, so you'll be able to go home shortly." He glanced at Frannie and Hiram, then at me. "Mrs. Edmundson, Mr. Cohen, Mrs. Chizzit. We want people to have a pleasant time when they come to Buckeye. I hope you'll try us again. He turned to Trooper. "Mrs. Hadley, the town was honored by your visit."

And he left.

If Trooper noticed that he hadn't invited her back again, she gave no sign.

By now the younger deputy was taking photos with a Polaroid camera. The older one approached our group, at the same time removing his dark glasses. He stowed them in his shirt pocket, taking his time about it, and studied each of us in turn. He drew out a notebook.

"Folks," he said, "which one of you owns the picnic basket this snake came in?"

Trooper acknowledged ownership.

"And you were the one who packed it this morning?"

"There wasn't any food in it. The food and champagne were all in the cold case." She gave him her best smile and crinkled up the corners of her eyes. "You see, I run tours— Trooper Hadley's the name, far-out travel's the game." She offered her hand, which he shook without much enthusiasm. "I keep the wicker basket on hand for celebrations," she went on. "It's all fitted out to hold champagne glasses and silverware around the sides, and there's a holder in the center for plates." She gave him the crinkle-eyed smile again. "But I didn't check it for rattlesnakes this morning."

He remained impassive.

"The hamper was in the back of that car over there," I

said, pointing. "We were all at the Buckeye City Hall watching a gold panning demonstration, and then taking photographs after the audience left. We weren't paying attention, and the hamper was right out in the open. There was at least a half-hour when anyone could have put the snake in there."

The deputy sighed. "Your name, ma'am?"

I told him. We went through the sequence of the afternoon's events.

When he finished taking our statements, he put his dark glasses on again and went back to the patrol car. The two deputies conferred and soon returned, the younger one carrying a large plastic bag. He stood holding the bag and gazing unhappily at the snake.

"It's prima facie evidence," the older one said, enunciating the Latin carefully. "We got to bring it in."

*We.* But salt-and-pepper mustache obviously had no intention of touching the snake. Rank hath its privileges.

The younger deputy made a move toward the rattler, which was still stretched out on the ground, then paused.

"I'll help you with that," Amos said. "You just hold out that bag, young man. And keep the top open."

The deputy, face averted, held the plastic bag at arm's length. Amos used his shovel to pick up the rattler's head and put it in.

"Oooh!" Frannie said. "Ugh!"

Amos set down the shovel and picked up the body, grasping it just below the rattles. The young deputy, still looking away, was not paying attention to how he held the bag.

"Open wide," Amos said.

The deputy complied.

Just as Amos was inserting the snake into the bag I heard the click of a camera shutter. I looked up to see Howie lowering the camera, a big grin on his face.

"Hot dog!" he said happily.

$\triangledown$

# 4

"WHAT WITH THIS rattlesnake business and everythin'," Trooper said after the sheriff's deputies had left, "I'm just wondering whether it'll be all right for me to stay in that motel room by myself." She was looking right at Frannie as she spoke. I noticed that her chin raised slightly and a smile tugged at the corners of her mouth. "Who-eeee," she said sadly. "I've had enough dangerous business for one day."

"Gracious!" Frannie exclaimed. "I've got a perfectly good guest room going to waste. There's no reason in the world why you couldn't stay with me."

"Who-eeee!" Trooper repeated—this time with enthusiasm.

Within moments, we were busy transferring Trooper's belongings from the Lincoln—hamper, cold chest, and all—into the capacious trunk of Frannie's Mercedes. Hiram looked more than a little disappointed. I was disappointed, too. I'd wanted time to talk with Jimmy privately and hadn't been able to. I'd come back to Buckeye another day, I decided.

"Gracious!" Frannie said once we were on the way back to Sacramento. "I've got to do some planning for supper. I had no idea we'd have such special company."

"Shoot, no need to go to any trouble." Trooper's drawl was still very much in evidence.

Frannie went on, ignoring Trooper's protest. "Let's see . . . I've got some shrimp bisque in the freezer; we can start with that. And I've been dying to try that recipe my sister-in-law Melissa gave me for roast beef salad with capers. We'll get some nice crusty French bread. And—of course!—ice cream for dessert."

"Just anything would be fine," Trooper said.

Frannie lapsed into happy silence, contemplating her plans for dinner, and Trooper began a story about one of her previous hurrahs. She kept up a raconteur role all the way to Sacramento, telling an hour's worth of amusing stories about eccentric and funny things her wealthy guests had done. At least she seemed to want to do something to merit the hospitality Frannie was lavishing on her—no matter that for Frannie the joy of providing hospitality was always its own reward.

As we approached our neighborhood, a well-preserved enclave of fine old houses and tree-shaded streets near Sacramento's downtown, Trooper studied our surroundings. We live at Twenty-second and U streets, in the heart of the neighborhood, and Frannie's well-maintained house with its tile roof and generous porte cochere spells M-O-N-E-Y. Trooper's lopsided grin was pretty broad by the time we turned into our driveway.

Frannie busied herself with supper. Trooper and I went to retrieve Trooper's belongings and rented car from her Sacramento motel.

I was impressed that she took less than five minutes to gather her things. She had very little in the way of toiletries and lingerie, and quickly fitted them into the side compartments of a small suitcase. From the closet she took a spare pair of slacks and a black jersey dress with a matching jacket, adding them to the contents of the suitcase. She put in a pair of high-heeled shoes, picked up a briefcase, and announced that she was ready.

After she'd checked out of the motel, we stood in front of her rented car—an economy model—while I began to explain the route back to Frannie's house in case we got separated in traffic. She paid little attention. The quirky smile was back, and the raised chin.

"Y'know, Emma, this seems an awful lot of bother—

havin' two cars." Her drawl was at maximum. "Seems t'me it'd make just as much sense to take this little car right back to the rental office tonight."

I remained silent, just to let her stew.

"Seems a shame to have that car clutterin' up your friend's driveway."

Still, I said nothing.

"After all, it's only until Tuesday," Trooper added.

"Suit yourself," I said.

We drove to the airport, where I waited while Trooper checked in her car. As she walked back toward the Mercedes I noticed that the limp I had spotted earlier had returned and was, in fact, more pronounced. Some long-standing condition, I supposed.

Back at Frannie's house, Trooper and I lugged the cold case and the picnic hamper in from the trunk of Frannie's car and put them in the hallway. Trooper busied herself unloading food from the cold chest into Frannie's refrigerator while I went to put the Mercedes away. I took time out to go to my apartment above the garage and check my answering machine. Salvage jobs had been scarce lately and I was hoping to find a message offering work. Nothing. One more week like this and I'd be hard put to pay my first-of-the-month bills.

When I got back to Frannie's, she and Trooper were happily chattering in the kitchen, Trooper dicing beef for the salad. I decided to check to see if anything more needed unloading from the cold chest or from the hamper.

The cold chest was clean as a hound's tooth, the lid propped open to let it air. I turned my attention to the hamper with the thought that we ought to run the glasses and plates through Frannie's dishwasher—the snake had been in here. I started to take out the delicate champagne glasses and immediately saw a piece of white paper, folded and tucked along the side. The deputies must have overlooked this, I thought. I plucked it out and was confronted by a drawing of a rattlesnake and a warning: "Don't tread on me."

I took it into the kitchen. "Look at this," I said to Trooper, and held it up.

She put down her knife and wiped her hands on a towel, then stared at it wordlessly.

Frannie peered over her shoulder. "Don't tread on me," she read aloud. Then she drew in her breath sharply. "Oh, dear!"

"A few kind words," I said, "from our friendly rattlesnake delivery person."

Trooper, tight-lipped, said nothing.

"How scary!" Frannie said.

"Garbage!" The word seemed to explode from Trooper. And, as if to illustrate her point, she snatched the paper from my hand and thrust it into Frannie's kitchen wastebasket.

"What's with you?" I said. "That's evidence!"

Without a word, Trooper went back to cutting up the beef slices, thrusting the chopped pieces carelessly into the salad bowl.

Frannie looked at me, worried.

"That's evidence," I declared again.

Trooper shrugged, retrieved the piece of paper, and stuffed it carelessly into her purse. "I'll turn it over next time I go out to Buckeye," she said. Turning away from us, she went back to the beef slices.

The dinner conversation began with Frannie's usual chit-chat, but soon we were listening to Trooper explain the progress of her various conservation projects—stories of wetlands and forests saved, archaeological sites preserved, and even an entire Mexican village saved from developers' bulldozers. But over Cherries Jubilee ice cream I brought up the subject of the "Don't tread on me" note. I point-blank asked Trooper if she had any idea who might be behind the incident.

She treated Frannie and me to a shrug and that quirky smile. "I never talk about misfortunes," she replied. "It's bad for business." And with that she excused herself and went upstairs to bed.

▽

# 5

We were lingering over one of Frannie's sumptuous breakfasts the next morning when I happened to glance out the kitchen window. An all-too-familiar car was pulling into the driveway. Dear Lord! Vince Valenti.

Vince is a retired cop. And a lifetime klutz with a talent for saying and doing the most awkward thing possible in any given situation. Not that he doesn't mean well—he is straight-arrow, true-blue, honest, loyal, hardworking, and all the other Boy Scout virtues. Also persistent. Much, much too persistent.

I've known Vince for several years. He's from Fairville, a small town halfway between Sacramento and San Francisco. It takes him an hour to drive here, and he'll come at the drop of a hat. I've never had the heart to tell Old Lonely to buzz off. Instead, I find some way to taper things down, ease him out of the picture. But Frannie's no help. Her matchmaker instincts always overcome her better judgment. I've pointed out to her over and over that it's not right to get his hopes up, summon him to Sacramento on one pretext or another; she's promised repeatedly not to do it again.

I glared at Frannie until I caught her attention, then pointed to Vince's dusty old Chevy. Frannie looked surprised. She wasn't faking it, I know her too well for that. "What on earth is Vince doing here?"

Trooper craned her neck to see out the window. "Who is Vince?"

"Um . . . a friend of ours," I said. "Vince Valenti. He's a former policeman."

Vince clambered out of his car. He reached back into the front seat, brought out a folded newspaper, and, with a somber look on his face, headed toward Frannie's side door. She jumped up to let him in.

Vince hurried into the kitchen, shrugging off his heavy jacket. He was sweating, and, as usual, was wearing ill-fitting, discount-store pants and shirt. Vince is long of torso and short of leg, and carries too much weight.

He came over to where Trooper and I sat at the breakfast nook table and presented me with this morning's *San Francisco Chronicle,* folded open to an inside page.

The photo Howie had taken ran prominently, under the headline "Gold Country Surprise for Adventure-Tour Leader." The young sheriff's deputy—a remarkable expression of revulsion on his face—held the plastic bag for Amos to deposit the snake. Trooper was clearly recognizable as one of the onlookers. So was I.

Vince spread the newspaper on the table and stared at me with anxious, china blue eyes. "Jeez, Emma! You coulda got bit. What were you *doing?*"

Old Lonely was incurable; any excuse would do. "Frannie and I were in Buckeye to see a gold panning demonstration," I said. "I'll bet the news story explains exactly what happened."

"Aw . . . you know, Emma. They don't always get these stories right."

"We went to see the demonstration," I repeated, "and then made the acquaintance of Trooper Hadley, who, by the way, is sitting at this very table."

Vince looked embarrassed. "Jeez," he said to Trooper. "I forgot my manners."

Trooper grinned at him and stuck out her hand. "Trooper Hadley's the name, far-out travel's the game."

Vince hurriedly shook hands with her, then ran his fingers through his sparse uncombed hair. "Jeez," he said again.

She reached for the newspaper. "Mind if I have a look at that article?"

"For heaven's sake, Vince. Sit down and have some breakfast with us." Frannie quickly adjusted our place mats to make room for Vince next to Trooper. "We'll get you set up in a jiffy," she said.

Vince reached out to the platter of cold cuts and cheese Frannie had provided with our breakfast. He took a piece of sliced ham, rolled it into a tube, folded it in half, and popped it into his mouth.

"Trooper is planning to stage a gold country hurrah," I said.

"Who-eeee!" Trooper clapped her hands with delight. "Just give a listen to what it says here, right at the end of the article. 'Hadley's presence in the Mother Lode country suggests she may be planning one of her exotic excursions for Northern California.' " She *who-eeed* again and tossed an imaginary hat into the air. "That Howie is *something!* Free publicity. My favorite kind!"

Vince reached for another slice of ham. "What's this country hurrah thing?"

Trooper happily launched into an explanation, repeating in detail the plans she had explained to Frannie and me: a stagecoach ride into town, Amos giving panning lessons and explaining the old-time mining methods, a camp-out alongside Tengold Creek with an evening's entertainment by an old-time melodrama troupe, and finally a departure from Buckeye by antique railway car.

As I listened, I reached over for the newspaper to have another look. Hiram's restored Lincoln was visible in the picture's background, and the story said Trooper was touring the gold country in an antique automobile—giving the impression the car was Trooper's. Was this Howie's doing? He'd presumably supplied the information that accompanied his photo.

Frannie came back to the table and placed a plate heaped with scrambled eggs and sausages in front of Vince.

"Thanks," he said. "I'm awful hungry. I just started

breakfast when I saw the news, so I came right away."

While Vince ate, Trooper continued her explanation of the hurrah plans, going into the preparations that would be needed. "I've got to get back to my place in Los Angeles right away to see about the railway car. The advance paperwork's goin' to be a nightmare."

"Gracious!" Frannie said. "I suppose so."

"I'll leave tomorrow. It's going to be a drag, managing everything from there. By the way, does either of you know about troupes that perform old-time melodramas?"

"There's the Drytown Players, and a new group in Columbia," I said. "And another in the town of Folsom. You could get a listing from one of the ticketing agencies."

"Um," Trooper said distractedly. "And findin' the right caterer is going to be a problem. Lordy! Stagecoaches, too. All these details . . ." Trooper turned her most enticing smile on me. "Emma, you know a lot about the gold country and I think you've got a special feel for this. I'd like to hire you as my assistant."

I was surprised she'd made the offer. At least she'd said the word *hire*.

"I don't know," I said. "Let me think." I wanted to say yes, just to be in on the creation of a fabulous Trooper Hadley hurrah. And I needed some money coming in. But Trooper's way of arranging to be offered favors bothered me. She had an on-the-edge quality I didn't like.

"Oh!" Frannie exclaimed. "Do it, Emma! I'll help you."

"Don't you think she'd be wonderful for the job?" Trooper said to Frannie. "And Emma's truck will come in mighty handy." She turned to me. "I'll pay mileage, too."

"I guess I'm for hire," I said.

"Who-eeee!" Trooper hollered. "We can talk about money later. Right now we need to get the wagons rollin'!"

I should have said no, I thought. We hadn't even settled on a rate of pay. But maybe it would be better to do that in private—I'd find a chance before she left for Los Angeles tomorrow.

Trooper asked Frannie for a writing tablet, and began a list. "This'll be the priority list for what I want you to coordinate," she told me. "I've already talked to Jimmy," she went on. "He'll do the publicity."

Damn! Jimmy was marching straight into the swamp.

Trooper glanced briefly at Vince. I caught sight of her quirky smile. "I'll need security, too, I suppose."

Vince, having finished eating, wiped his hands thoroughly on his napkin. "You just put down on your list what you want me to do," he said to Trooper. "I'll do it for free."

"Terrific!" Trooper said without looking up. Not-so-terrific, I thought. She was using Vince, too.

He shifted importantly in his chair. "You ladies got to have someone to take care of you. That snake in the picnic basket, somebody's got to check into that."

"Maybe Vince could take that warning note and get it properly turned over as evidence," I said to Trooper.

She glanced up in annoyance.

Vince looked alarmed. "What warning note?"

"Last night we found it in the picnic hamper," I told him. "A plain piece of paper; it looked like it came from a copy machine. It had a warning and a drawing of a snake."

"Omigosh!" Vince said. "I got to know what happened with this snake business—start to finish."

Frannie and I filled him in on the details while Trooper continued to scribble in her notebook.

"I'll get on it today," Vince said. "The sheriff's guys got to have that note." He glanced at his watch. "Jeez, the morning's half gone, and I gotta fill in for one of the Fairville guys on a four-to-midnight. But I can make it down to Buckeye and back first."

Trooper sighed, then fetched her purse and handed Vince the note. He made a big show of getting a plastic bag from Frannie and putting it in. "They're not gonna like this— weak chain of evidence. But with me delivering it, I guess it'll go down all right."

After Vince left, I took another look at the newspaper

article. "You know," I told Trooper, "there's something here that bothers me. This article gives the impression . . . well, it leave Hiram out and implies the car belongs to you."

"No harm in that." She gave me the twinkle-eyed smile. "Publicity's publicity."

"But Howie may be intending to sell the picture elsewhere. To travel magazines maybe."

"No harm done," Trooper insisted. "I need all the ink I can get." She favored me with a grin and a wink, then gave her shoulder a wriggle in a credible imitation of Mae West. "It's the perception that counts, m'dear."

Frannie giggled.

I was more uneasy than ever about having agreed to work for the great Trooper Hadley. And, as things worked out, I didn't get the chance to talk money with her until the next day when I took her to the airport.

She'd busied herself with her notepad as we drove, working from yesterday's notes to write separate lists for Vince, Jimmy, and me. After I'd parked in the loading zone to drop her off, she handed over copies of the lists. "I've put my Los Angeles phone number on each of these," she said, talking fast. "So if you want to know—"

"I'd like to know something now," I said. "How much were you thinking of paying me?"

"Well, now . . ." The drawl had instantly come back. "For the mileage, just charge me whatever you charge your salvage customers."

"How about my time?"

"Ah . . . let me think." Trooper tucked her briefcase under one arm, then reached for her little suitcase. I leaned across in front of her and took hold of the handle of the passenger door. I didn't open it.

"Let's base your pay on a daily rate," Trooper said. "Plus expenses," she added.

So far so good.

Trooper glanced pointedly at her watch. "I can't give you the amount per day until I get to my office. I'll have to project expenses and profits contingent on sign-up for the trip."

This was getting sticky. I couldn't actually hold her hostage. I pushed open the door.

Trooper started to get out, then turned to me. "If we get a good sign-up," she said, "I'll give you a bonus for helping handle the extra people." She hitched the briefcase more securely under her arm, slid most of the way out of the truck, and then again turned toward me. "Sorry, sweetie. This is the best I can do."

By the time I had pulled the truck door closed, she had hurried through the big glass doors into the terminal. I sat staring after her, not certain what irked me the most: not being told what I would earn, or being called sweetie.

# 6

$T$HE NEXT MORNING, Wednesday, I headed out toward Buckeye at eight o'clock sharp. It was too early to let Jimmy know I was on the way, but I figured he wouldn't be too surprised when I showed up. Trooper had told me he'd be expecting me midweek to coordinate our work.

The drive would take an hour or more, plenty of time to think about Jimmy's situation and whether to report anything to his mother yet. I could certainly understand his yen to work with the famous Trooper Hadley—I'd succumbed to the temptation myself. But it wasn't as risky for me; I had no job at stake, no family to support.

I kept to the slow lane as I traveled south, mulling over Trooper's behavior and at the same time enjoying the early spring vistas—an occasional marshy pond left from the winter rainy season, here and there a scattering of meadowfoam on the lush grasses. When I reached Highway 18 I headed east toward Buckeye, starting the steady but slow ascent to the Sierra foothills.

The two-lane road was deserted, flanked by grazing land. It must have looked the same for decades, I thought: the narrow, tar-patched roadway, the sagging barbed wire fences, the occasional clump of scrub oak. This was a backwash, a left-behind place. I liked it.

Eventually I passed the old school where we'd had the encounter with the rattlesnake, and crossed the railroad track. Highway 18 continued straight ahead; I turned left and went up Buckeye Boulevard, which looked to me to be the original Route 18.

Just beyond the intersection was a chamber of commerce sign: "Welcome to Buckeye, Where Old and New Meet." Hanger boards announced meetings of the local Rotary Club and the times of services for several churches. Another board, attached at the top of the sign, touted a Labor Day rodeo.

Half a block up Buckeye Boulevard, on the left, was Marie's Doughnut Shop. It had all the earmarks of an old A & W Root Beer stand. There was a small kitchen building with a sales window and some indoor seating, and a roofed-over walkway leading from it, flanked by outdoor tables and benches.

On the adjacent hillside were small houses of mixed vintage scattered at random angles. One, a rambling house perched king-of-the-mountain style on the highest part of the slope, caught my attention. It was oversize for the neighborhood and exhibited a collection of the excesses of 1950s suburbia—faux-stone siding across the front, kitsch-board trim on the porch, and, on top of everything else, wrought iron in the instant-Colonial tradition. I wondered who'd put that monstrosity together.

Up ahead was City Hall Drive, where Frannie and I had turned off to go to the panning demonstration. The road was as new as the building itself. The pavement was shiny black; the recently painted lines stood out sharply. I drove on past, following Buckeye Boulevard into the older part of town. After several blocks, I was in the nineteenth-century downtown.

I slowed to enjoy the sights, savoring the names of the businesses: Abe's Hardware, Model Pharmacy, New Pine Cone Cafe, Gemini's Appliances. The buildings were in the distinctive style of gold rush country, with tall, narrow windows and doors, iron shutters, and even the occasional pilaster or granite facade. Only a few of the storefronts had been modernized: tile-fronted in the 1920s, or, more recently, cheaply board-and-battened for an "Old West" appearance. I saw few pedestrians.

The offices of the *Buckeye Bugle* were in an old building with black-painted iron pilasters on the front. I parked, went inside, and found myself confronting an old-fashioned high counter, the top painted brown and the front faced with tongue and groove in a dingy gray. No one was in sight.

I sounded the "Ring for Service" bell on the counter, waited, and rang the bell again. Jimmy, looking anxious and harassed, emerged from the back of the building. "Oh, shoot!" he said when he saw me. It seemed the *Bugle* came out on Thursdays, so that on Wednesdays Jimmy had a three o'clock deadline. He'd have little time to spend with me.

"Debbie—she's our front-counter girl—isn't supposed to take a long break when I'm putting the paper to bed," Jimmy said, "but I guess she did."

"There's just the two of you here?"

"Yeah," he said. I caught a tone of resentment in his voice. "She does the counter, the classified ads, and sometimes the routine obits or weddings. I do all the rest."

Just like I used to do when I worked with Jimmy's mother, I thought. But in this office I sensed none of the camaraderie I'd once shared with Adelaide. And when Jimmy'd said "I do all the rest" he sounded unhappy. I could well imagine his duties: the nighttime meetings—city council, planning commission, chamber of commerce, school board. Also PTA carnivals, Rotary Club pancake breakfasts, and you-name-it. His mother had done it for years.

"We can go out for a quick cup of coffee when Debbie gets back," Jimmy said, "but I've got to finish some darkroom work first." He took off his glasses and polished them with the fabric of his cardigan sweater. Without the glasses, Jimmy's unfocused eyes gave him a childlike appearance. But resentment gave his voice a sharp edge. "My boss, Oliver Piccard, has a screaming fit whenever something isn't ready on time. He runs that printing plant of his on a split-second schedule."

Behind the counter was a stairway that I'd assumed led downward to a print shop. I indicated the stairs. "Isn't the paper printed here?"

"Years ago it was, but when Piccard took over the printing operation went modern." Printing operation and modern were emphasized with scorn. "Nowadays, what the *Bugle* is all about is printing contracts. The new plant's up at Leona, the county seat."

"Your publisher has other printing contracts?"

"Damn right."

At that moment a plump young woman in blue jeans and a sweater scurried in.

"Oh, gee! Sorry, Jimmy. I didn't mean to be so long."

"I've got to get a few prints out of the rinse tray and into the drier," Jimmy said to me. "Then we go for coffee."

I waited until he returned.

"The Pine Cone is just about our only option," he said, "unless you want to drive to the doughnut shop. Or the motel, but I wouldn't recommend that."

"The Pine Cone's fine."

Over coffee we quickly reviewed an announcement Jimmy had written of Amos's next demonstration. It would be Sunday; he planned to explain the use of a Long Tom.

"I've got some great photos of Amos with the Long Tom he built," Jimmy said. "He knows a lot about old-time mining things. You ought to see his barn. He's got great stuff in there."

Jimmy's enthusiasm was in remarkable contrast to the resentment he'd shown earlier. I wished I could just pat him on the back and say: Forget your job on the newspaper. Do something you enjoy, like promoting Amos and the hurrah.

"Howie's going to be working on the hurrah," Jimmy said. "He's agreed to do it on spec."

I had to admire Trooper's audacity. She'd rounded us all up, offering to pay only if she had to. I wondered what she'd promised Jimmy. I came close to asking as we walked back but decided to wait and see what he'd tell me.

Jimmy paused to lean against one of the iron pilasters outside the *Bugle* office. He glanced up and down the street. "You know something lucky about last weekend? Amos decided to take us outside the city limits, to the old schoolyard."

"Why was that lucky?"

Jimmy jerked his thumb in the direction of City Hall. "How do you think our friend Palooka would have handled the rattlesnake business?"

I had no idea, and said so. "But I had the impression your city manager would rather forget the whole thing."

"Right. He doesn't like what Amos is doing, drawing attention to historic sites on land he wants to make into a discount mall. And you can figure his reaction to Trooper's gold country hurrah. A few dollars from the tourist trade are nothing compared to the megabucks he expects to rake in."

Jimmy *was* in deep trouble. No two ways about it: the small-town newspaper editor who wants to keep his job goes along with the pillars of the community.

"You're putting yourself in a risky position," I said to Jimmy.

He shrugged. "It gives me a kind of a satisfaction, seeing how close I can shave it. You know, Oliver Piccard is in tight with McCready. The two of them have a couple of real estate deals cooking. Besides, Piccard's a"—he glanced behind him, as if his boss might be listening—"gold-plated asshole. Sorry for the language, but that's the truth."

I waited, hoping to hear more.

Jimmy glanced up and down the street again. "I've got to get back to work."

"One more thing," I said. "You see the police reports, don't you? Did Palooka write up the snake incident?"

"No. And I got my orders from Piccard to keep it out of the *Bugle*."

▽

# 7

THERE HAD TO be more to Buckeye than I'd seen so far. Wemmer's car agency, for instance. I decided to explore a little further, follow Buckeye Boulevard on through town; I imagined it would slope downhill again at the east edge of town and rejoin Highway 18.

The old downtown ended within a block of the *Bugle* office, its farthest limits marked by a sturdy concrete block building labeled "Buckeye Volunteer Fire Department." Several residential streets branched to my left, one graced with a "School Zone" sign. Undoubtedly, this was Buckeye's main residential area, the newer houses.

I followed Buckeye Boulevard, which indeed curved downhill and rejoined Highway 18. At the intersection was the Buckeye Motel, built in the old auto court style—a row of cottages joined by flat-roofed carports. Near the highway was a newer structure, with the motel office and a restaurant—the Yellow Lantern. It had two entrances. One, near the motel office, bore a sign declaring it to be a coffee shop. The other faced Highway 18. Its "Restaurant and Lounge" sign featured a martini glass outlined in blinking neon.

I turned right on Highway 18 and headed back toward the west, where presumably I'd be back at the intersection with the chamber of commerce sign. The highway was bordered by open land until I came to an old ranch site on the south side. It had a modest house and a large, well-maintained barn. Playing a hunch, I slowed to check the name on the mailbox by the driveway: Amos Fugaldi.

I considered what might be stored in Fugaldi's barn. Saddles and horse-drawn vehicles, maybe. Certainly old tools and mining implements, and probably lots of antique farm equipment. Maybe, I thought, we could use some of it to dress up the hurrah.

Next on the south side of the highway was a rodeo arena, and after that was Wemmer's car agency. It had a big lot—a row of shiny new cars and trucks at the front and an empty, grass-grown expanse at the back. There was a small sales hut, atop it a sign as big as the structure itself: "Wemmer's Autos and Trucks. Buckeye's Best Buys." The remainder of the premises consisted of a service bay and a repair shop.

I drove on, until I'd passed the intersection with the chamber of commerce sign and arrived at the Nye schoolyard, where I turned around. I went back, up Buckeye Boulevard and up City Hall Drive, and parked at the far edge of the City Hall lot, intending to have another look at the mining sites Amos had pointed out last Sunday.

The field on my right was dotted at regular intervals with grass-covered mounds of dirt. Amos had said these were made by Chinese rockers, used whenever gold could be found close to the surface. "The rocker looked like a baby's cradle," he'd explained, "with a box on it at the head end, and riffles leading down from that. The miner shoveled dirt into the box, ladling water out of a barrel and rocking the cradle." Amos had pointed out that the rows of rocker tailings were always easy to spot. "The miner would use stakes and string to mark off squares," he'd said. "Then he'd go right down the row, mining each square."

My gaze traveled beyond the Chinese rocker site. On a far hillside were more mounds. Why hadn't Amos pointed these out? At first glance, I thought they were made by Chinese rockers. But they were different in size and proportion, the spacing less regular. I'd have to ask Amos about them, I decided.

To my left, curving behind City Hall on a gentle downslope, was Chinaman Creek. Beyond, in the far distance, was a sight I'd been familiar with all my adult life: dredger tailings—rocks and gravel stacked in great piles, some as high as a one-story house.

The enormous gold dredgers that made them used to be a common sight in the lower foothills. They traveled slowly across the land like grazing dinosaurs, taking with them their pond of water. Their continuous-bucket chains—each bucket as big as an elevator car—dug into the ground ahead of the dredger and the dug-up material was fed into a revolving perforated drum that ran the length of the dredger. Paydirt and small gravel washed through the perforations, and the gold was collected by means of cleat boards mounted on shaker tables on each side.

Consolidated Mining was one of the biggest dredger companies, Amos had said. "They got their start and were headquartered in Buckeye, but they bought up land everywhere for mining." I wondered if Consolidated still owned all that land covered with piles of gravel. How much land around Buckeye *did* the company own?

According to Jimmy, Jonathan McCready had been the local manager for Consolidated before they went out of the dredging business. When the mining operations ceased, he'd chosen to stay in Buckeye and become its first city manager.

A smart choice. It gave him access to the inner circles at both Consolidated and the city of Buckeye. And, clearly, he had the brains to take full advantage of his position. I filed the thought away, with the addendum that he probably also had the resources to make life difficult for anyone who got in his way.

By this time I was ready for a cup of coffee and some lunch. Plus, I hoped, a little gossip. I decided against going back to the New Pine Cone Cafe; the waitresses would be too busy for conversation. The Yellow Lantern held no appeal. Marie's Doughnut Shop was it.

Behind the counter at Marie's was a stubby woman with a grease-stained apron around her middle. She wore her frizzy gray hair in a topknot. Her eyebrows and complexion were as colorless as her hair and she had pale gray eyes. In contrast, her mouth was a bright red slash of lipstick. She'd taken my order for a hamburger, poured my coffee, and slapped the patty of meat on the grill without a wasted motion. Now she stood openly studying me, at the same time wiping a damp cloth in slow-motion circles on the countertop.

I kept my silence, hoping she'd start the conversation. She didn't. "Are you Marie?" I asked after a while.

She laughed. "Hell, no! There never was no Marie—the name's Agatha. But you ain't gonna run no successful business called Agatha's Doughnut Shop, now are you?"

"My name wouldn't work either," I said, and stuck out my hand. "I'm Emma."

"Guess not." She wiped her hands on her apron and shook hands with me. "By the way, you just call me Aggie."

"Glad to," I responded.

Aggie turned, then flipped over the hamburger patty and began arranging a bun, lettuce, and pickle on a paper plate.

"You had this place long?" I asked.

"Twenty years next summer." She grinned at me, the laugh lines at the corners of her eyes joining the latticework of fine wrinkles that crisscrossed her face. "Honey, it's no worse than bein' married." She chuckled, then glanced toward my truck at the rear of the parking area. "A-1 Salvage. You got your own business, too?"

"I sure do."

"But you're not working here in town."

"No, I'm not."

She served up my hamburger, adding a packet of potato chips to the plate, then leaned back, hands on hips. The question was unspoken. So what are you doing here? I was pleased with myself for having chosen to come to the doughnut shop. Aggie was probably Gossip Central for Buckeye.

"Work's been a little scant lately," I said. "So I decided to enjoy the time off. I haven't been up in this neck of the woods for a long time."

"It's pretty in the springtime, ain't it?"

"Sure is." I started in on my hamburger.

"Hotter'n the hinges in the summer, you know what I mean?"

"You bet. I hate to work on days like that."

"But that's when we get the tourists. Damn fools trottin' up and down Highway 49 in the heat—some come down here, too. I do my best business in July and August."

"How about the man who does the gold panning demonstrations? Think he'll pull many tourists?"

"Old Amos?" She picked up a spatula and began scraping the grill. "Him and his junk? He's been collecting it for years. Humph! All his talk about *historic* sites. Maybe some college professor'd come out here to look at his lumps and ditches; your regular tourist won't." She shook her head. "People shouldn't come around encouraging him. The old coot's crazy enough as it is, especially since his wife died." Aggie looked at me suspiciously. "You come out here Sunday for that gold panning thing?"

"A lady I work for wanted to see it," I said. "She doesn't like to drive on the freeway, so I drove her over from Sacramento."

Aggie gave a last emphatic swipe with her spatula, moving the greasy debris into a channel at the front of the grill. "So what did you think?"

"Well, I learned something about panning for gold."

Aggie refilled my coffee mug, then poured some for herself and came around to the front of the counter to sit beside me. "Were you there when that out-of-town gal came in the old car?"

"Yes, I was."

"Well . . . ?"

"I don't know much about Trooper Hadley, except that she does excursions for rich people."

"Yeah, them whatchamacallits—hoorays. So what did you think of her?"

"She's . . ." I fished for an answer that didn't take sides. "She's certainly an attention-getter."

"I know. I heard about them pants. And that hat." Aggie paused, gave me an appraising look. "You know about the rattlesnake."

It was true-confession time. No way out of it—news travels fast in a small town and she might know more than she was letting on. "I was there," I said.

"Hot damn! No kidding?" Her pale eyes sparkled. "Who do you think did it?"

"Lord knows. Maybe some kids."

"Must have been out-of-towners. We got some wild kids in Buckeye, but none of 'em would do a thing like that."

"I suppose not," I said.

"We don't need no out-of-towners to promote Buckeye. Most of all we don't need that Hadley woman comin' here, tellin' us how to run our town." Aggie's topknot of frizzy curls quivered with indignation. "And her morals are no better than they ought to be, if you know what I mean."

"It sounds like you know something I don't know."

"Damn right. That woman was here before the gold panning demonstration, tryin' to snuggle up to Bill Wemmer—he's the chamber of commerce president."

"Oh?"

"My sister, she works a morning shift down to the restaurant by the motel. Now, that's a shady place, but the breakfast crowd is okay. Matter of fact, it's the only place in town serves breakfast—I only do doughnuts and coffee and the Pine Cone don't open till nine." Aggie snorted. "From lunchtime on . . ." She turned to look at me. "You know what people in Buckeye call that motel? The riding academy, that's what."

I worked to suppress a giggle; Aggie leaned forward confidentially.

"You know, my sister said that Hadley woman let Bill Wemmer take her there for lunch."

I couldn't help but defend Trooper. "Maybe she didn't know what kind of place it was."

"Or maybe she just didn't like the cut of Bill Wemmer's jib."

"What do you mean?"

"Well," Aggie admitted, "maybe I shouldn't be too quick to judge." She slowly wiped her hands on the front of her apron, as if begrudging the movement—also any qualification of her opinion of Trooper. "In all fairness I got to say it. My sister told me she up and walked out on Wemmer halfway through the lunch."

$\triangledown$

# 8

THE MESSAGE LIGHT on my answering machine was blinking when I got home. It was Vince, asking me to call him.

He picked up his phone on the first ring. "Hullo?"

"It's me—Emma."

"Jeez, I'm glad you finally got home. Emma, you got to go over to the sheriff's office in Leona."

Now what? He was bustling with self-importance.

"You got to go over there and sign a statement about the note with the snake on it."

"How come?"

"Well, rules of evidence—secondhand stuff isn't good enough. They took a statement from me, but it's gotta be from you because you found the note."

Vince launched into a chain-of-evidence explanation, putting a lot of police jargon into it. I tuned him out, still musing about the Wemmer-Hadley tête-à-tête.

I tried to imagine what had happened. Wemmer probably saw to it that they were seated in a dimly lit corner and tried to push drinks on Trooper. Trooper would be smart enough to refuse a drink, then do her best to keep the conversation businesslike—she would want to keep a surface-friendly relationship with the chamber of commerce president. And Trooper could easily fend off a little sexual banter, a few innuendos. But she'd gotten up and walked out. Wemmer must have done something downright crude.

"Isn't that right? Emma?"

"What? Sorry, I was distracted for a minute."

"Like I said, we gotta be careful with these backwoods types—make sure they take that statement right."

I sensed what was coming: the inevitable invitation.

"So, how about I come pick you up tomorrow first thing? We'll go over there together."

"Vince . . ."

"We could have lunch afterward, maybe."

"No, Vince. I can't do it."

"Aw . . ."

"I've got to meet with Jimmy Simpson—you know, the editor of the *Buckeye Bugle*—and with his photographer friend, to go over plans for the hurrah."

"Well, some other time. Okay?"

"Sure," I said casually. A mistake.

"Hey! How about Friday? They got a place over in Leona serves great cheeseburgers."

Bulldog Valenti never gives up. Or takes a hint.

"We'll have to see, Vince." Time to change the subject. "Say, what did you learn about the investigation at the sheriff's office?"

"Those guys couldn't find it with both hands—'scuse me for saying that." Vince was in top bristling-with-indignation form. "They don't think this is important. The only one that cares is that young deputy with the mustache."

"I remember him. The snake-shy one."

"Yeah. New on the force, a real hotdog."

"I don't think it would do any harm to have someone taking this seriously."

"Well, this hotdog's barking up the wrong tree. He says that Hiram guy could have been the target just as much as Trooper, because it was his car. Jeez! I tried to straighten the kid out—you know, tell him what you said about Trooper being a lightning rod."

I found myself trying to remember how much I'd told Vince about my interpretation of the local politics. My version of what was going on—or, worse, Vince's—might not play well with the folks in the county seat.

"Tell me what else you told him . . . this hotdog."

"I told him what happened at the gold panning demonstration and all, just like you told me." And Vince started in, with almost word-for-word recall, beginning with Trooper's arrival in the old car.

I decided I needed to know more about Buckeye politics, even if I had the general gist of it. Aggie seemed like a sure source. Gossips are all alike: moralistic. Judgmental. Monitors of the status quo, ready to report who was violating it or might be about to. And she'd applied the old double standard to Trooper's adventure with Wemmer at the Yellow Lantern. She represented the conservative community opinion. Mistrust the outsider. A pox on any changes that aren't brought about by Buckeye's own.

Vince had reached the end of his recital and suddenly changed conversational course.

"What do you think, Emma? Maybe we oughta be barking up a few extra trees ourselves."

"How so?"

"If that hotdog sheriff's deputy can go by the book, maybe we should, too—not write off any suspects."

"You think maybe Jimmy Simpson did it? Or his friend Howie?"

Vince was always oblivious to sarcasm. "Okay. We got Simpson, and the photographer—no, we don't. They was with you the whole time. That leaves them out. Also Amos."

"Don't forget, that leaves out Frannie and me, too."

"Huh? Aw . . . Emma!"

I felt guilty for teasing him. "Well, if you assume the snake was planted before Trooper and Cohen arrived at the demonstration—"

"You got Trooper and Cohen as suspects. Uh. Wait a minute."

I waited. Vince was getting out his notebook. I imagined him carefully marking down names. I was certain Hiram Cohen hadn't manhandled a rattler into a picnic basket. But Trooper? She could, in all likelihood. But why on earth would she?

"So what's next?" Vince asked.

"Let's think about what happened after the audience—including some of Buckeye's notable citizens—left the panning demonstration."

"Their names?"

"Bill Wemmer. And a chiropractor named Truesdale—and his wife—plus the city manager, Jonathan McCready."

As I spelled all the names for him I decided I needed to know more about Mrs. Truesdale, and whatever it was between her and Trooper. I wondered if they had met earlier in the week or if it was some previous connection. Whichever—neither wanted to acknowledge it.

"I got to start checking into these Buckeye people," Vince said.

"And one more thing. I want you to check into Trooper's background."

"Huh?"

"It's something you can do that I can't. Use your connections to get a line on her—finances, that sort of stuff."

"Aw, Emma, you don't think—"

"I don't think she's the guilty party," I told him, "but I think we need to know more about her."

"Okay. Spell her name for me."

"H-A-D-L-E-Y."

"And you're not gonna forget about signing the statement for the sheriff's guys in Leona."

"I won't forget. I'll do it first thing in the morning."

The next morning I was out early. By nine o'clock I'd finished in Leona and was headed toward Buckeye and a planning session with Jimmy and Howie.

But when I arrived at the *Bugle* office I learned Howie wouldn't be there. "He had a stroke of luck," Jimmy explained. "Some big corporation in San Francisco wants him to go to Merced and photograph their new fertilizer plant—a hurry-up assignment."

"I suppose that's good luck," I said, wrinkling my nose in mock disgust.

Jimmy laughed. "Fertilizer's big-time stuff down that way. Don't knock it, it brings in the bucks." He sighed, suddenly mournful. "This is a real break for Howie. Mileage, expenses, top rates . . . plus he gets a bonus if he can finish by Monday."

"Sounds like it pays better than newspaper editing."

"You know it." Another sigh. "Photographers just make more than writers. Howie and I have this partnership going on the side. Photojournalism. I scout the stories and place them. Then I do the writing; he takes the pictures."

"So how's it going?"

"We did okay on a piece about bed-and-breakfast inns in the Mother Lode country, except they paid twice as much for the pictures as for the copy." He took off his thick-lensed glasses and started polishing them, staring unseeingly over my left shoulder.

"And . . . ?"

"And after that, zilch." He put the glasses back on. "I spent a lot of time scouting stories and writing query letters. And I haven't got a damn thing to show for it." He sat up straighter in his office chair. "Except my wife was madder 'n hell over the money that went for letterhead and postage—and all the time I wasn't spending with little Jimmy."

"Surely your wife would understand—that you need to earn extra money, I mean."

"I haven't exactly told her what's going on. I was offered a profit-sharing plan here. But it's a fizzle." He chuckled humorlessly. "A profit-sharing scam."

Now we were getting down to it, I thought. "Tell me about this profit-sharing thing."

"Piccard doesn't believe in sharing." Jimmy leaned forward. "Look, here's how he works it. There are two corporations, both of them owned by the Piccard family—the newspaper and the printing operation. The only decent-paying spot on the newspaper is selling ads; Piccard's cousin does that and makes fat commissions."

This was the trouble his mother had sensed, I was sure of it.

"The printing operation is Piccard's," Jimmy went on. "It makes all the money. Besides the *Bugle*, it prints the *Tengold Daily Nugget*, a bunch of little weeklies, and even one of those throwaway shopper news things that's distributed in Stockton."

"Doesn't the *Bugle* ever make a profit?"

"Never. Piccard would have a cow! Any time the *Bugle* looks like it might bring in a little extra cash, he raises the rate for printing the paper or ups the commission for his cousin."

He put his head down on his hands. "Sooner or later I've got to tell my wife about this."

"Why haven't you?"

"Well . . ." Jimmy seemed to be searching for the right words. "Joyce's parents—you know—have a lot of money. She's never had to cope with anything like this. Besides, she's got enough problems already—lonely and blue because I'm gone a lot—she hasn't been able to find women friends in Buckeye she has much in common with." He sighed. "And last week the doctor confirmed what we suspected. This time we're going to have twins."

"Congratulations," I said automatically.

"Yeah, sure."

Silence.

"Damn Oliver Piccard all to hell!" Jimmy kicked viciously at his wastebasket. It overturned. He stooped, ostensibly to right the wastebasket and pick up the spilled papers, but I could see he was trying to hide his feelings. He didn't look at me, but made a job of cramming papers back into the wastebasket.

"I take it your salary here at the *Bugle* isn't exactly munificent."

He finished with the wastebasket, straightened, and then deliberately leaned back in his desk chair. "Hardly." He managed a wry grin.

"But you took the job anyhow."

"Yeah." He shook his head sadly. "That was last fall, back when I was living in Ignorant City. Joyce and I thought we'd make it because of the profit-sharing plan and a lower cost of living here. Back then we told ourselves this was a real Norman Rockwell kind of place. You know, a gentle, friendly small town that would be just right for raising kids."

"And?"

"I should have checked into it," he said bitterly. "We suspected Joyce was pregnant. I knew I was going to have a bigger family to support." Jimmy's fists were clenched. He was worried about his family, of course. But he'd been humiliated, too; Piccard had put one over on him.

I took time out to give some thought to Piccard. What made him so chintzy? Sheer greed, more than likely. But also the naïve young editors he hired wouldn't stick around for long. There wouldn't be any inquisitive outsiders to get the long-range picture of his other transactions, or those of any of his real estate buddies. I made a mental note to ask Vince to use his connections to check into Piccard, too.

# 9

JIMMY WAS EAGER to show me his plans for publicity for the gold country hurrah. He wanted the chance, I thought, to prove his competence. And I again noticed how happy and enthusiastic he was, in contrast to his mood as editor of the *Bugle*.

I was impressed with what he'd done—outlined a basic no-frills publicity plan, and augmented it with a list of extras that could be undertaken if Trooper could come up with the money. He also had schedules for picture taking and news releases, and on top of that he had already written the publicity for Amos's presentation next Sunday. Amos was to show the operation of a Long Tom as well as repeat his panning demonstration.

It was nearly noon by the time Jimmy gathered up his plans for the hurrah publicity and tucked them into a battered briefcase.

"How about lunch?" I asked. "I'll treat you to the best the New Pine Cone Cafe has to offer."

"Sounds better than the cheese sandwich I had stashed in the office refrigerator," Jimmy said. "But let's do it this way—you advance the money and we'll put it on the hurrah expense account."

"Why not," I said, giving no hint I had any doubts about Trooper's finances.

"Oh, shoot!" Jimmy exclaimed after we were seated at a booth near the back of the Pine Cone. "*He's* here."

"Who?"

"Piccard."

I turned around to look. Sitting with the man who had to be Oliver Piccard was Buckeye's city manager and primo real estate investor, Jonathan McCready. I had a good stare until a flicker in McCready's expression told me I'd been recognized. I turned back quickly.

I wondered just how rich McCready and Piccard were. It likely didn't matter; they'd want to be richer. And I knew the contemptuous attitude held by most developers: you could have what I have if you were willing to work as smart and as hard. And opposition to development was seen as merely the bleatings of out-of-power fools. It never dawns on men like this that pavement isn't better than pastures, or shopping centers aren't an improvement over land in its natural state. They didn't see the negative side to development— that it erases the past and messes up the environment.

McCready was again dressed in a well-cut but out-of-date suit, with a white shirt and conservative tie.

Piccard was no equal to McCready in either looks or wardrobe. He slumped in the restaurant booth; his knitted shirt fit awkwardly over his narrow shoulders and slack physique. A mop of wavy brown-gray hair topped his craggy features. His skin was pasty.

"Piccard doesn't look the martinet type to me," I said.

"You oughta catch his act sometime. From him, the highest form of praise is absolute silence."

"Tell me about the real estate deals he and McCready are into."

"I understand they made a killing on some former Consolidated land out near Rancho Murietta. And have more properties up near Sacramento they're planning to sell."

The waitress came and we gave her our lunch orders.

By this time McCready was engrossed in writing in a leather notebook. Piccard was talking to him, rapid-fire, jabbing a small calculator into the air to emphasize his points.

"Piccard isn't involved with McCready's annexation deal, is he? I mean the one with Truesdale and Wemmer."

"No. Piccard's been here only seven or eight years." He grinned. "A relative newcomer. McCready's partnership with Truesdale and Wemmer goes all the way back to the seventies."

That opened up a new line of conjecture. "It's hard to hold on to a piece of real estate that long," I said. "I wonder how they've done it—paid property taxes and other costs, with nothing coming in."

"They sold the city a small portion of the annexation tract some time ago, the land for the new City Hall, which must have taken care of things for quite a while. Still, I think they've had problems recently. You can look at the whole annexation story for yourself. I've got a file folder full of clippings, plus the legal notice for the annexation hearing that ran in this week's *Bugle*. I'll lend the stuff to you when we get back to the office."

"Thanks."

We fell silent as the waitress brought our lunch.

"I imagine the news articles speak in glowing terms of the proposed annexation," I said to Jimmy after she'd left, "with not a word about opposition to it."

"Right. They were written to prescription."

"Well, who opposes the project?"

"If any of the Buckeye citizenry wants a slow-growth policy here, I haven't heard about it. I guess old Amos is the only fly in their ointment—or was, before Trooper arrived on the scene."

"And that's only because Amos thinks the gold mining sites should be saved?"

"Every damn ditch."

"And you don't think so."

"Not really. In my view Amos wants the right thing for the wrong reason. I'd hate to see this town given over to car lots and discount malls. But . . ." Jimmy shrugged.

"Isn't there historical value to the mining sites?"

"Academic types seem to like them. Someone came over from the University of the Pacific—the California Confer-

ence of Historical Societies is headquartered there—and
then several history groups came on field trips. I guess that's
what got Amos stirred up. And there's also the Chinese
Diggings. You haven't seen it yet. It's spread out for acres on
those fields the other side of Chinaman Creek. Amos says
the kind of mining they did there was called ground sluicing.
It's kind of complicated to explain; there's a network of deep
ditches. They used Chinese workmen there, hundreds of
times."

"Sounds impressive," I said.

"For a while it had our big-time developers a little worried.
Representatives came here from the Chinese Historical So-
ciety in San Francisco. They brought in this expert from
China, some kind of international expert on historical archaeology."

"Then what happened?"

"Nothing. Everybody more or less ignored it and the whole
affair slipped into limbo."

"Are there any other mining sites around here?"

"Well . . ." Jimmy grinned. "There's always the dredger
tailings."

"But you can't put them in a museum," I said. "Any more
than you could that ground sluicing site."

"That's the trouble. The stuff is quite literally all over the
landscape. You can't scoop up all this stuff and put it in a
museum."

Still, I thought, you could take the perspective that the
sites were even more valuable because there were so many.
With enough funding the area could become a state or national park. But enough funding was impossible these days.

The waitress brought our check, which I picked up.

Jimmy grinned at me. "What else do you want to know?
You've fed me, I'll tell you anything."

"Trooper fed us," I said, with more confidence than I felt.

Jimmy gestured toward the front of the restaurant. "Well,
there they go." McCready and Piccard were heading toward
the door.

I paid for our lunch and we emerged in time to see McCready's big Chrysler pulling out of a parking place across the street. Piccard was in the passenger seat.

"Looks like they're headed for City Hall," Jimmy said.

"Any particular significance to that?"

"Nope. It's standard operating procedure around here—developers and city manager, incorporated, doing business as usual."

We walked in silence for a while.

"They don't worry about appearances?" I asked.

"No. They're just so damn smug—totally smug. They can't imagine running into any serious opposition."

Jimmy lowered his head, a stubborn set to his mouth. I was struck by the movement, so similar to the way his mother used to react. "Trooper's a good contender for that role."

"You, too, Jimmy. Take care. You could lose your job."

"So?" Jimmy lowered his head even further. "I'm tired of these jerks always saying they don't want people from out of town telling them how to run Buckeye."

When we got back to his office Jimmy dug out the file folder with information about the proposed annexation. I thanked him again and headed for my truck, eager to get home and look over the details of the developers' plans.

As I approached, I saw something white stuck under the windshield wiper. "It couldn't be," I said softly to myself. But when I unfolded the paper I saw the now-familiar snake and "Don't tread on me" message.

I was shaken. Before this I had felt safe. I had been a spectator, an outsider, merely an interested bystander and not a player in the drama. But now I had lost my amateur status.

$\triangledown$

# 10

I FISHED IN my glove compartment and brought out the envelope in which I usually keep gas receipts—the only place I could think of to keep the note safe. I stuffed the receipts in my pocket and, careful not to touch the sheet of paper in any new places, put it into the envelope.

I headed for the sheriff's office in Leona and was halfway there before I realized that this time the note belonged with the Buckeye police. But I didn't want to stop and turn around; I didn't want to hand it over to Palooka O'Rourke. My imagination filled with images of the treatment he'd probably afford this new piece of evidence.

His reaction would be unreadable; he'd look at me with those eyes squeezed almost shut by his fleshy cheeks. I could see him accepting the gas-receipt envelope and taking the warning note out with his ham-size hands, giving no thought that he was leaving his paw prints all over it. In fact, I imagined, the note likely would be in the wastebasket the moment I was gone.

Jimmy had told me Palooka was good mainly for keeping order at the high school games. I couldn't see him as *Detective* O'Rourke, and, in fact, wondered how he'd qualified for the police force in the first place—he didn't seem very bright. I suspected his only talent was doing what McCready wanted. I knew I shouldn't pass judgment on the man, but I kept on toward Leona. The note belonged there, I told myself, as part of the sheriff's ongoing investigation.

I'd finished my business at the sheriff's office and headed

back toward Highway 18. I decided to stop in downtown Leona when I spotted a sign in the window of a sporting goods store. They had topographic maps—just what I needed to interpret the information about the real estate deal. I bought a map of the Buckeye area and went into the coffee shop next door.

The topo map was magnificently behind the times, its most recent revision in 1967. Par for the course—you never find one that's up-to-date. I glanced at it briefly, as I started sipping my coffee, then turned my attention to the file Jimmy had given me.

A recent article from the *Bugle* carried a banner headline, "Annexation Proposed," and a smaller head, "Buckeye to Increase in Size Three Times." This was a much bigger project than I'd supposed. With the story was a map showing an area that extended all the way from the railroad track to undeveloped land east of the Buckeye Motel, and from south of Highway 18 to well north of Chinaman Creek.

"The Tengold County Local Agency Formation Commission has at long last given approval to the largest annexation in Buckeye's history," the article read. "The developers, Buckeye residents Jonathan McCready, Cecil 'Doc' Truesdale, and Bill Wemmer, say they plan a prompt groundbreaking for an auto plaza anchored by a new Wemmer's sales site, with work on a brand-name discount mall and an industrial park to come soon after."

The auto plaza—"a regional bargain park of auto agencies"—was to be located on a strip at the north edge of Highway 18. Wemmer's sales lot would occupy the prime site, the first lot after the railroad tracks.

Auto sales bring big tax revenues, but car buyers from the big city don't always materialize. I wondered that Buckeye's movers and shakers could be so confident; Buckeye was a long way from anywhere.

How could Wemmer et al. ignore the failed auto mall at Hallock City down in the Sacramento Delta? I'd seen what happened there. Fine old pear orchards and a good-sized chunk of wildlife habitat along the river's edge had been destroyed. And for what? Plywood covered the windows of the abandoned showrooms; the cold fog wind from San Francisco Bay swept debris across empty sales lots.

I wondered what inducement the city of Buckeye might offer to persuade car dealers to locate here, and found the answer two paragraphs later: McCready had gotten a legal opinion that the city could use its redevelopment funds to construct a large electronic sign on Highway 18 to advertise the dealerships.

I supposed it would be placed to the left of Highway 18— not far from the railroad tracks, and perhaps where the little home-grown-looking chamber of commerce sign was now. But it would be many times as tall. I closed my eyes, trying to imagine the sign. It would be close beside the road, its thick concrete legs planted on the hillside like some modern-day Colossus. It would be a desecration in that rural setting, its message board endlessly blinking time, temperature, and sales messages.

It would be altogether out of place, I thought. But then I reminded myself that the setting would change. Wemmer's new sales lot would replace the grassy hillside, graded and paved. And the new auto row would back up against the scattered, miscellaneous houses that now dotted the slope, with the far corner of Wemmer's lot probably adjacent to the ill-designed king-of-the-hill house. But I supposed anyone who would choose such a style deserved what they got.

I glanced quickly at the rest of the news story.

Land along the railroad tracks from Highway 18 to the north side of Chinaman Creek was slated for the industrial park, presumably to take advantage of the now-disused railroad tracks. Land to the east of the proposed industrial park, the tract of rolling hills behind Buckeye City Hall, would be transformed into the discount mall. Damn! This was where most of the mining sites were to be found.

I folded up my newspaper and map, planning to take a further look at all this at home. As I drove back toward

Sacramento I wondered if the developers would be able to start anything besides Wemmer's new sales lot very soon. But maybe, to mix a metaphor à la Vince, they had something up their sleeves they were playing very close to the vest.

The immediate problem was the potential for conflict with the gold country hurrah. Trooper had talked about having her group camp along Chinaman Creek, perhaps on its lower reaches where it joined Tengold Creek near the intersection of the railroad tracks and Highway 18. Trooper's happy campers would be screened from the town by a ridge of low hills, but a new Wemmer lot under construction wouldn't add anything useful to the ambience of the trip.

When I got home, in late afternoon, the blinking light on my answering machine told me I had a message. I hoped it would be from Trooper. She'd said she'd let us know when she'd be coming back from Los Angeles—she'd more or less promised to be here by tomorrow.

But the call was from Sam Jones, of Spicer Realty in Roseville. I called the number and a disinterested female voice came on the line right away—beyond doubt an answering service. Mr. Jones would return my call promptly, she told me in a bored tone.

Surprisingly, he did.

"This Mrs. Chizzit? A-1 Salvage? Sam Jones here, Spicer Realty."

"What can I do for you, Mr. Jones?"

"Oh, I imagine you'll be mighty pleased when you know what I want. I got a job for you."

I *was* pleased with the prospect of a job. But most clients don't start out by saying I'll be happy to have the work. "What did you have in mind?" I asked, trying to keep my voice suspicion-free.

"A nice little cleanup job in the south area, a piece of property that's going to be put on the market. Yes, ma'am. I think it's just the ticket for you. A friend of mine told me about you, said you do real good work."

"Oh?"

"Real good work. That's what he said."

"That was very nice of your friend."

I paused, hoping he'd mention the friend's name. He didn't.

"Whoever it is, I'd like to thank the person," I prompted.

"I'll pass the word along, Mrs. Chizzit. Yes, ma'am. Now, this work needs doing right away."

"How big a job is this?"

"Just right for you, I'd say. And it's out in Sacramento's south area—do you know the old Portuguese Hall out on Riverside Boulevard?"

"Sure." The hall was a fine turn-of-the-century building, one of the few remnants of an old rural community.

"Well, we haven't put a sign up or anything, but we've got an out-of-town buyer coming to look at it—want to have it in just-right shape."

We. Jones spoke as if he and a partner owned the building.

"Can you start tomorrow, Mrs. Chizzit?"

"Well, I usually look at a site first and then give my bid on the job."

"Oh, we don't need to do that. Just go ahead and do the job tomorrow, then bill me. Yes, ma'am. Do the job tomorrow. Bill me. That's Sam Jones, Spicer Realty, 3041 Jefferson Street—"

"Wait a minute! I don't do business this way, Mr. Jones."

"Well, surely, you could make an exception, seeing as . . ."

"I don't make exceptions. In any event, I've got something else I have to do tomorrow morning. But I could meet you there tomorrow afternoon and bid the job then—maybe start the first of the week."

"Oh. Well. Suit yourself."

I put on my ending-the-conversation voice. "Okay, Mr. Jones, I'll meet you. Portuguese Hall on Riverside Boulevard, two o'clock tomorrow afternoon."

He agreed and we bade each other goodbye.

What an out-of-kilter conversation! I couldn't decide what the man was up to, and wondered whether he'd try to stiff me—he was awfully glib with the just-bill-me stuff. No matter. I could probably sort this out when I met with him.

I got out the 1967 topographic map and again began trying to locate things on it. It showed City Hall downtown, next door to the Buckeye Volunteer Fire Department. Also, the present route of Highway 18 was marked with dotted lines and labeled as a proposed route.

I tried sketching in the mining sites, but without the new City Hall for reference I had trouble matching the contour lines on the map with what Amos had shown us—the gently sloping hillside where Chinese rockers had left their piles of debris, and also the inexplicable mounds on the farther-away hillside. I was more curious than ever about these; as nearly as I could determine they abutted and possibly overlapped a site marked "Old Cemetery." There must be something wrong with my interpretation of the location, I thought; the mounds didn't look like gravesites and I couldn't recall having seen a cemetery up there.

I sat for a while, frustrated, then decided to see what I could learn about Wemmer, Truesdale, and McCready at the neighborhood library. I arrived shortly before closing time, and pulled out a Buckeye phone book. I was in luck. All three developers had addresses listed, which I looked up in the library's collection of local maps.

Wemmer lived on Wemmer Road, south of town—apparently at exactly the spot designated on the topo map as "Old Wemmer Ranch." So the family weren't newcomers to the area. And Wemmer, with a family-owned chunk of real estate—on top of his share of the land to be developed—was probably well on his way to becoming a very wealthy man.

McCready's home was in a subdivision northeast of town, the farthest out on a curving street that led beyond the high school. No doubt it was one of the town's nicer residential areas. The McCready place would be discreetly upscale, I was sure, but not ostentatious.

I found myself quite interested in Truesdale's address. If I'd interpreted the maps correctly, he lived in the garish, king-of-the-hill house. Interesting.

I put the phone book and the maps back in their places, then stood for a moment, lost in thought about Mrs. Truesdale. A curious lady she, married to a Willy Loman type like Truesdale and, apparently, willing to live in that awful house. Plus she had some connection with Trooper that neither of them wanted to acknowledge.

$\triangledown$

# 11

FRANNIE HAD INVITED me to supper the next evening—
Friday—which was when we finally heard from Trooper. She
phoned to say she had too much to do in Los Angeles and
wouldn't arrive until Sunday morning. And she said not to
pick her up at the airport; she'd arrange her own transpor-
tation to Buckeye.

"Gracious," Frannie exclaimed, "she certainly must have
a number of things to tend to. But I don't understand how
Trooper plans to get to Buckeye from the airport. Do you
think we ought to meet her flight, just in case?"

Frannie suffers from what I call compulsive hostess syn-
drome. "No need to go out there on a maybe-so," I told her.
"Trooper can rent a car and drive to Buckeye in plenty of
time for Amos's demonstration. It doesn't start until two
o'clock."

"Mmmm," Frannie said, which meant she was reserving
judgment.

My thoughts were still occupied by the puzzling behavior
of Mr. Sam Jones of Spicer Realty. We'd met that afternoon
as scheduled. He'd rummaged through his pockets for a moment before finding the keys, then let me into the long-aban-
doned hall. He stood to one side, seeming both impatient
and disinterested, while I looked the place over.

"You want the outside tidied up, too, Mr. Jones?" I'd
asked. "I'll be happy to cart off the fallen branches in the
little orchard around back, trim the hedges—you know,
make the place look maintained."

"Sure, sure. Put it in your bid."

The whole affair was crazy. The building needed only a good housekeeping. I could probably sweep it out, brush the dust off the windows, and collect the stray bits of trash in little more than a half-day. Ditto on time required for the outside. This must have been obvious to Sam Jones. But he didn't bat an eye when I gave him a bid based on two full days' labor—plus an extra fifteen dollars I tacked on out of perversity.

"My secretary will have a check ready for you when you're done," he'd said. And walked away without a backward glance.

"I still can't figure out that business with Sam Jones," I said to Frannie.

"Gracious!" She shook her head. "Don't worry about good fortune, as the Chinese say. Here, have some more fettuccine. And clam sauce, too. I made it myself."

"Okay." I accepted a second helping of everything—fettuccine and sauce, green salad, French bread. And still I puzzled over Sam Jones's odd behavior.

The next morning, Saturday, Vince phoned. "I picked up some dope on Trooper, but not much," he reported. "Say, is she around? I want to go over security plans with her."

"She's not here, Vince. She postponed coming back until morning. She'll go directly to Buckeye from the airport."

"Aw . . . how we gonna figure security? Like you said, she's a lightning rod. She's gonna attract trouble."

I wasn't in much mood to worry about Trooper's protection. "What information did you pick up about her?"

"It's more like I *didn't* pick up any."

"Okay. So what did you *not* learn?"

"It shoulda been easy. You know, just a computer check. DMV. Real estate taxes. Whether she's voted lately and where she's registered. Stuff like that."

"And?"

"I didn't find out much, except she's voted in just about every election, and even got absentee ballots for the times she was planning to be out of town. Other than that . . .

nothing. No accidents on her DMV record. No property taxes, so she must rent the places she lives in. Doesn't own any other real estate, either."

"How about her business situation?"

"I didn't get time to check out that stuff, but I put my friend in the department working on it—credit rating for her company, Trooper's Hurrahs, plus loans to the business. Or real estate or other stuff owned by it."

I was going to be interested in what Vince's friend managed to dig up. "Maybe Trooper has all her assets in the business," I said.

"Yeah. Maybe."

"What do you mean?"

"Maybe there ain't no assets."

That didn't sound plausible to me. But it was consistent with Vince's modus operandi: go for the obvious. "I wonder if there are other ways to get information. For instance, what about the people who went on her River Boat Ramble?"

"Yeah . . ." I could also hear the wheels going around in Vince's head. This was exactly the kind of work he does best—plodding, hang-in-there stuff. And, as often as not, Bulldog Valenti makes it pay off.

"You could start with Hiram," I said.

"Yeah. *Great* idea!"

I knew Vince would be off and running. And, I hoped, out of my hair for a while.

I'd no sooner hung up than Hiram Cohen phoned, wanting to talk to Trooper. He was surprised she wasn't coming back before tomorrow.

"I just don't understand it. She said she'd be here Saturday—today. She said to bring the car, we'd go out to lunch. So I drove on up."

I was tired of trying to figure out why Trooper had delayed her return and was in no mood to answer questions about her motivations or plans.

Trooper could do her own explaining. I gave Hiram her Los Angeles phone number.

$\triangledown$

# 12

"ISN'T THIS EXCITING!" Frannie exclaimed, for what must have been the tenth time that Sunday morning. She'd been ready ahead of time and was waiting by the driveway even before I'd backed the Mercedes out of our garage.

As we drove down Highway 99 she kept up a steady stream of comments, her brown eyes sparkling with anticipation. "Isn't this a glorious morning? Oh, I'll be so glad to see Trooper again. Do you suppose Hiram will come and bring his car? Oooh, I can hardly wait to find out about Amos's Long Tom!"

"Amos will tell us all about it," I assured her.

Undoubtedly, and despite his protestations he'd watch audience reactions more carefully this time. We'd coached him to keep the length of his talks within the attention span of his audience. Still, I expected he would take a full half-hour to explain the workings of a Long Tom. Not that it's all that sophisticated. It's just an extended sluice box—a series of flat troughs linked together and set up on stilts. Water flows in at one end, the miner shovels in pay dirt, and gold-bearing muck collects in riffle boards nailed to the bottom.

Frannie abruptly stopped chattering. "Oh, Emma! You haven't said a word for miles—you're being such a glumpot! What's wrong with you?"

"I'm sorry, Frannie. I've been . . . um . . . thinking."

"You are not! You're *stewing*."

"You're right," I conceded. "I hadn't wanted you to worry, but I'm afraid something might go wrong today."

"What, for instance?"

That was exactly the problem. "Lord! I don't know."

"You don't have to bite my head off."

Frannie brushed at her jacket as if ridding herself of invisible particles of my ill temper, and then settled into a new position. "Shame on you. And *you* were telling *me* not to worry about how Trooper would get to Buckeye. Don't go borrowing trouble. It's a gorgeous day."

It *was* a beautiful day. Last week's cold winds had abated, replaced with capricious warm breezes. The scene around us was right out of a picture book: puffy white clouds, blue sky, green grass, clusters of yellow mustard. And there were plum trees in bloom and patches of China lilies to mark the places where old houses once stood.

We pulled into the parking lot behind City Hall a few minutes after nine o'clock and found Amos hard at work. He'd apparently just finished setting up the Long Tom and had dug a ditch to it from the creek across the field. Parked at the ready was a wheelbarrow full of dirt.

Amos gave us a friendly wave and then, as we watched, pulled open a wooden gate at the bottom of his miner's ditch, allowing a sun-sparkled stream of water to flow through the Long Tom.

Frannie immediately began clapping. "Bravo!" she yelled.

"I intended to have something more," Amos said, "but I suppose it will wait for next week."

"What something more?" I asked.

"A stagecoach."

"Goodness! A *real* stagecoach?"

"Yep." Amos pushed back his hat. "The exact same stagecoach as used to come over the Tengold grade, up until . . . let's see, I think it was 1920 they replaced it with the high-wheeler truck."

"This is the same stagecoach?" I asked.

"Yep. Bill Wemmer's cousin had it, kept it in a barn out at his grandpa's place. But when they was putting in the new highway the barn had to go. He didn't know what to do with the stagecoach—that and a whole lot of other stuff. I told him not to worry, I'd take it off his hands." Amos straightened, then pulled his hat forward and settled it at a more businesslike angle. "Now I can't say it was the same stagecoach used in the earliest days, but it's the one they had just before they got the truck."

I wondered if we were in for a dissertation on stagecoaches.

"I been going to get that stagecoach fixed up for years," Amos went on, "but I only started this past winter after . . ."

He sighed, looking away from us and across the rolling green hillsides. After his wife died, I surmised.

"Well," Amos said briskly. "I thought I'd have more spare time. But I'll have her ready to roll next week."

"Gracious, Amos! What an enormous lot of work you've done."

"It wanted doing anyhow," Amos said.

"Could we see the stagecoach?" I asked.

"Sure thing, soon's I finish a couple things here."

So Amos did have a barnful of equipment. The good citizens of Buckeye surely didn't understand the valuable resource they had in Amos Fugaldi and his "junk."

"By the way," Amos said. "I'd be obliged if you ladies didn't mention that I've been readying the stagecoach. I don't like to promise and not deliver."

Frannie promised.

"I'll keep quiet about it, too," I told Amos. "And I want you to know I certainly admire all the work and knowledge you've put into this project."

At that moment Howie pulled into the lot in his old station wagon. With him was Jimmy Simpson. Howie waved at us with great energy. "Who-eeee!" he hollered, imitating Trooper's yell.

Howie and Jimmy hurried over to examine the Long Tom. "Who-eeee and hot dog!" Howie whooped, spacing out his words with an exaggerated drawl. "Just lookee at this here photo opportunity."

Frannie giggled.

Amos, looking decidedly pleased with himself, went over to the Long Tom and struck a nonchalant pose.

"Perfect!" Howie exclaimed. "Absolutely perfect!" He hurried to his station wagon and began rummaging through his camera equipment. "When's Trooper going to get here?" he hollered.

I shot an inquiring look at Jimmy. He shrugged.

Howie returned with a light-reflecting umbrella and his largest camera case. He handed the reflector to Jimmy, took a camera out of the case, and paused—apparently to consider which lens he wanted to attach.

"How was your fertilizer expedition to Merced?" I asked.

Howie put on a look of mock concern and held a finger to his lips. "Shhh! Don't breathe a word. I'm supposed to still be there."

"Ah!" I said, falling in with his mood. "But you're not taking pictures of the fertilizer plant. You're here."

"Absolutely." He laughed.

"Did you finish your assignment?" I asked, going back to my normal tone of voice.

"I sure did!" He again fell into conspirator mode, looking around as if searching for possible eavesdroppers. "Don't tell the folks who hired me. The only thing that took time was getting shots of the executives, who think I am—at this very moment—slaving away in my darkroom. They believe I will scarcely have my prints made in time to go back to Merced this evening for some night shots."

"And," I went on for him, "you will again slave in your darkroom, working almost until dawn."

"You got it! At which time I will leave for San Francisco to present the finished work, putting it in their hands in the nick of time to collect a hefty bonus."

"Here comes Trooper," Frannie announced.

We turned, suddenly aware of the whine of the old Lincoln's gears. The top of the car was down; the canvas and cobalt blue paint sparkled. Trooper sat beside Hiram, wearing her Aussie hat and red sweater. She hollered a full-vol-

ume "Halloo!" and clambered down from the car to stand
with her hands on her hips admiring the Long Tom.

"Absolutely authentic lookin'. And a real miner's ditch to
bring the water. Amos Fugaldi, you are a wonder!"

He grinned, at the same time blushing.

"And Howie's here, too," Trooper went on, still in full cry.
"Howie, glad to see you."

Was I glad to see Trooper? I tried to make up my mind.

"Howie, come right on over here," Trooper said. "We got
us some picture taking to do."

After the photography was done, Trooper took me aside to
tell me that my salary, on top of expenses, would be $100 a
week. "Part-time work, mind you. Don't keep track of time.
Just decide for yourself what needs doing."

It was small wages, but I was hooked—intrigued by the
situation in Buckeye and by the enigma of Trooper's personality.

Trooper hadn't even waited for my assent. "Hiram,
honey," she drawled, "why don't you bring out that big coffee
jug, and the cups and fixings."

Hiram and Amos brought out the picnic hamper, making
elaborate pretenses of checking for rattlesnakes before they
opened it, and we stood around in the spring sunshine with
steaming cups of coffee, exchanging news of developments
since the week before. Still, after a while Trooper pulled
Jimmy to one side for serious conversation. They were at it
quite a while. My nagging doubts about Trooper returned. I
could get by with the small amount paid—I had other
sources of income and only myself to look out for. But with
Jimmy it was different.

Amos's yelp took us all by surprise.

We turned to see him standing by the Long Tom, one hand
raised and his fingers stained with a dark substance. "Oil,"
he cried out in dismay. "Someone's loaded my Long Tom
with oil!"

# 13

Rᴵɢʜᴛ ᴀᴡᴀʏ I started looking for a "Don't tread on me" note and found it—a neatly folded square of white paper tucked under the wiper blade on the far side of Amos's truck. I asked him if the note could have been there when he un-loaded his shovel and gold pan from the truck.

He paused. "Mebbe so."

"How about you, Howie?" I asked. "Did you see anything when you got out your camera gear?"

"Nope. I wasn't looking, anyhow."

Trooper reached for the white piece of paper. "I suppose we ought turn this over to the sheriff's men."

"Good," I said. "Let's not destroy any fingerprints, and put it in something for safekeeping."

Trooper didn't touch the note, but leaned back against Amos's truck with an air of patience-beyond-all-reason. Still, when we couldn't find anything to put the note into, she volunteered one of her linen napkins.

"That'll do it just fine," I said.

When Trooper spoke again, her drawl was so thick you could have sliced it and made sandwiches. "Hiram, honey, would you fetch one of those napkins from the hamper?"

Howie stepped forward, camera in hand. "I'll take a pic-ture of it under the wiper blade."

"Good thinking," I told him. "Take pictures of Amos's Long Tom, too, and show the oil dumped in it."

"It's of no use now," Amos said sadly. "I'll have to break it up, throw it away, and start over."

I remembered what he'd said last Sunday, that when someone dumped fish oil in a miner's equipment, the man would be smart to get out of town.

"Before you do anything with the Long Tom," I said to Amos, "I think the deputy from Leona ought to have a look at it."

But what could the deputy possibly find? I couldn't imagine any fingerprints would remain on that rough wood.

"Couldn't we just set this thing to one side?" Amos asked. "Then I could get another one put together in time . . . not as good, but . . ." He turned to Trooper. "What do you think?"

"I don't think you can finish a new Long Tom in time," I said. "In the first place, we've got to wait for the deputies to come over from Leona, then—"

"Why do you think you have to have the sheriff's deputies?" Jimmy asked. He gestured at the City Hall building. "Like it or no, we're within the jurisdiction of the Buckeye Police Department. It's in the basement there, just around the corner."

I hurriedly shifted mental gears, feeling like a fool. Of course, you couldn't get much more within the city limits than where we were.

"I'll notify the local authorities," I said, feeling absolutely no enthusiasm for the task.

My journey across the parking lot and around the corner to the police entrance seemed to last forever. I took it slowly, dragging my feet, literally and mentally. As I walked I thought of the image I'd conjured up earlier of Palooka, how he'd behave if I brought evidence to him. His eyes would be implacable in those larded cheeks; he'd stuff the evidence carelessly into a plastic bag, intending to do nothing with it. There was something stupidly atavistic about Palooka, a stubborn regression to a primitive ignorance. No. I was reading too much into the situation, letting my imagination run wild. Still, it was with great reluctance that I pushed open swinging doors that led into the police department's reception area and walked up to the counter.

Palooka sat at a desk by the back wall. He took his time getting up, deliberately creasing and folding the newspaper he'd been reading. He still held it under one arm as he lumbered toward me. With deliberate care, he set the newspaper down on the front counter.

"Help you?"

He had to have recognized me from last Sunday. Annoyed at being treated like a stranger, I explained about the oil in the Long Tom and the warning note. My temper rose moment by moment as Palooka listened to my recital, his small emotionless eyes revealing nothing. But then, as I neared the end of my explanation, I began to wonder why I was so angry. I'd dealt before with people who were a great deal less civil, and not lost my cool. Palooka was, after all, only a small-town salami—overweight and ill-qualified for his job. Why was I making him a target?

I wasn't so much angry at Palooka, I realized, as at the role he played. He was McCready's lackey, the developers' pawn. And, just like Aggie, he represented the insular, smug people of Buckeye—implacable in their certainty that their values were the only ones worth having, incapable of seeing any reason to preserve their town's heritage. I was angry at them, because they couldn't conceive of a legacy to leave their children other than a fat bank account. They'd put car lots over historic sites, and profits before anything else, apparently intent on creating a tenth-rate San Jose along Highway 18.

Palooka's voice intruded on my thoughts. "Is the Long Tom and everything else still out there—in place as it was?"

His voice was surprisingly harsh.

"Yes, it is," I told him. "Well, mostly. We took the note out from under the windshield wiper."

He heaved a prodigious sigh, a wordless complaint against the physical effort I had imposed on him. Then he trundled back to his desk to push a button on the telephone, and collect a notebook and a Polaroid camera.

My animosity toward Palooka vanished; I couldn't believe

I'd been so angry at the man. He was only trying to earn a living, carve out the best niche possible for someone in his circumstances.

"What kind of oil was in the Long Tom?" he asked.

I tried to bring back the visual memory of Amos's hand as he held it up. "Not clear like salad oil," I said. "Dark."

"Crankcase oil, maybe?"

His voice was still harsh. Why was he questioning me? All he had to do was go outside and take a look for himself. As if reading my thoughts, Palooka—without waiting for an answer—pushed through the entry door and headed for the parking lot.

The newspaper he'd been reading was still on the counter. I told myself it was probably the present-day equivalent of the *Police Gazette*, some publication with sleazy cheesecake photos and lurid crime-scene depictions. Or maybe it was one of those tabloids you pick up at the supermarket check-out counter.

I took a look. It was the *Wall Street Journal*. Maybe, I told myself, he'd found it in McCready's office.

A pile of reading material was neatly stacked at the upper left corner of Palooka's desk—a newspaper and several magazines. I went over for a look and was dumbfounded to discover yesterday's *San Francisco Chronicle*, folded to the editorial page, a *New Yorker*, and two library back-issues of *Scientific American*.

$\bigtriangledown$

# 14

Nᴏᴛ ʟᴏɴɢ ᴀғᴛᴇʀ I'd hurried to follow Palooka out the door, a heavy hand landed on my shoulder. I jumped, startled.

"Emma! I been looking everywhere for you."

Vince. I'd wondered why I hadn't seen him sooner.

"We gotta talk. I got all this stuff to tell you."

"Like what?"

He took time to mop his glistening brow—Vince always perspires. "Look . . . uh . . ." He glanced around, ignoring the commotion that was still going on about the Long Tom. "We could sit in my car and talk."

Vince opened the car door for me, his usual show of courtesy, and then hustled around to the driver's side. Before he'd even settled in his seat he was fishing in his shirt pocket for his notebook. "I checked around," he announced. "Got a line on Wemmer and that McCready guy and the doc—Truesdale." He tapped a stubby pencil against his notebook, obviously pleased with himself.

"Now we're getting somewhere," I said.

Vince flipped the pages of the notebook. "We start with last Sunday. I checked whereabouts for everybody."

"And?"

"To begin with, Wemmer's clean. Let's see. Wemmer . . . last Sunday . . ." Vince was still flipping pages. "Okay. I got it. Wemmer was at the agency. Showed up around ten-thirty ᴀ.ᴍ., his usual time, and was there all day except for when he came to the panning demonstration."

"Vince, are you sure he couldn't have stayed a little overtime? Maybe just long enough to—"

"Not a chance. He cleared out when McCready and the
Truesdales did. I got him verified back at the agency; he had
an appointment to show one of their new four-wheel-drive
vehicles to a local rancher."

"Rats!"

"Huh? Oh, yeah. You wanted some dirt on him."

"He was my best choice," I said. Wemmer, for me, sym-
bolized Buckeye's collective smug insularity.

"Like I said, not a chance for him to do something," Vince
insisted. "And ditto for today. He showed up at the agency
at ten-thirty. That's where I was this morning. And just now
I talked to Amos. He said he checked that Long Tom thing
at eleven and it was okay. So that puts Wemmer out of the
action. Twice. Still, I don't trust him."

"Why?"

"Gossip around town has it that he let some guy—Mexican national—run cockfights on the Wemmer ranch. There
was a lot of talk about it, because the sheriff's men raided
one of the fights without giving the usual notice to the Buckeye police. Some people said the sheriff was right. Others say
he was wrong."

"Sounds to me as if there wouldn't be a cockfight to raid
if the locals knew about it in advance."

Vince nodded. "Sure. I seen that kind of stuff before."

"Anything else on Wemmer?"

"One more thing. He and his wife split some years back.
There was a legal hassle because he didn't want to give her
money she was supposed to have, something about his ranch
getting more valuable during the time they were married. He
didn't think he should have to pay up."

"Maybe he wanted to forget California is a community
property state."

Vince shifted in his seat, scratched his thinning hair.
"Well, I could see how he'd feel about that."

There was an uncomfortable silence between us.

"Still and all," Vince went on, "that weren't no cause to hit her—a man's got to be pretty low to do that."

"He hit his wife?"

"Yep. Right after the judge said he had to pay."

"Is the lady still around town?"

"Nope. She took off. Nobody knows where she is."

"So that leaves us with Wemmer as a minor sleazeball. With a hot temper."

"Yeah. He had a motive to get Trooper out of town but no opportunity."

"So how about the rest of them?"

"No luck. The Truesdales and that McCready guy are tied up in a tidy package—all of them out of the picture. They got together after last week's demonstration to play bridge, Mrs. McCready included. And that's what they was doing right up to the time McCready got a phone call about the rattlesnake thing."

This sounded interesting. "Who made the call?"

"That Buckeye cop. Palooka. He's got standing orders to call McCready when anything happens."

"How did you find out about the call to McCready?"

Vince grinned, pleased with himself. "Oh, I talked to lots of people around town."

"You've been to Marie's Doughnut Shop, I bet."

He looked at me, mildly surprised. "Yeah. I talked to that Aggie there."

"Me, too," I admitted. "She doesn't think much of Trooper. What else did you learn?"

"Well . . ." He turned notebook pages. "There's not a whole heck of a lot on McCready. He was the local manager for Consolidated before he became city manager."

This matched what I'd learned from Jimmy. "Or, more precisely," I told Vince, "he decided to ensure himself a good situation for some long-term real estate investing."

"Yeah. He's a slick operator, what I heard."

"And probably too smart to involve himself in any skulduggery."

Vince sighed. "Right."

"What did you learn about Truesdale?"

"Truesdale? He does a lot of his socializing over at Leona, the county seat. He's big in the rod and gun club there—got himself some fancy marksmanship awards. And he's in the sheriff's mounted posse."

I hadn't known they still had those honorary posses. But Tengold County might.

"Also, Truesdale's what you could call a ladies' man—worked his way through chiropractor school as an Arthur Murray dance instructor. Furthermore . . ." He made a show of consulting his notebook again. "We got a lot of disagreement among the locals about how many times he's been married."

"No kidding?"

"Yeah. The first marriage was for twenty years. Then he was out of town for a while. Rumor had it he found himself some rich widow to marry. Anyhow, he was gone for a long time. But he was a single man when he finally came back to town. Then last year he went away on one of those cruise ships and brought this new lady with him. Folks around here don't know much about the current Mrs. Truesdale. She keeps to herself."

Vince scratched his head. I recognized the signal. Something was bothering him, something he couldn't quite put his finger on.

"Did you find out anything about her?" I asked, thinking about the odd exchange of glances with Trooper.

"She's a real nice lady," Vince told me, his china blue eyes gleaming with enthusiasm. He scratched his head again, still trying to cope with qualms of some sort. "You know, I got the idea she's maybe kind of lonely. Seemed like she really wanted to talk to me."

"Oh?"

"I don't know who she was talking to that she knew I was asking questions, but she spotted me on the street and asked me to her place for coffee."

Curiouser and curiouser.

Vince went on. "You know, Mrs. Truesdale is a real lady."

"How so?"

"It's just how she dresses and talks and all." Vince ran a hand through his thinning hair.

"There's something here you don't understand?"

"Yeah. It's hard to put it to words. The Truesdales live in this big house—the biggest in their neighborhood. But for her, that neighborhood . . . well, she don't match the neighborhood, that's all."

"I know the house. You're right."

"Yeah. A lady like her belongs in a different kind of place—maybe a big old house with lots of lawn and tall trees. You know, like maybe she grew up rich."

Not a bad description of old money.

"Maybe a big house in a whole neighborhood of big houses—that's where a lady like Mrs. Truesdale belongs."

"You could be onto something, Vince."

"Sure. The house looks okay for him, the doc. Just not for her. He's a chiropractor, which I guess isn't the same . . . not as fancy as maybe a regular doctor might be."

I stopped to consider the situation. I didn't see it quite the same way as Vince. There was something too studied about the woman's pastels and pearls and her Grace Kelly elegance. The more I thought about it, the more certain I was. Mrs. T. didn't quite cut the mustard for having been to the manor born. Rather, she dressed as if she were playing the part for an audience—a Buckeye audience, who wasn't the sort to distinguish the finer nuances of the genuine old money crowd. I wondered what she was doing married to a type like Truesdale, and what she'd done before she came to Buckeye to play tasteful lady.

And, for that matter, why she'd been pumping Vince.

$\triangledown$

# 15

By two o'clock that afternoon the City Hall lot was nearly filled by people who had come to see Amos's demonstration. Most of them waited at the back end of the parking area, admiring Hiram's car. Trooper lounged nearby, chatting with all comers.

I counted the house. We had forty or so, a good showing. They were mainly out-of-towners, Sunday tourists with cameras around their necks. Still, some locals had shown up; I recognized a few faces I'd seen at the New Pine Cone Cafe.

I considered the Buckeye attitude, as enunciated to me by Aggie at Marie's Doughnut Shop: Outsiders who tried to interfere in local affairs were not welcome. Trooper was the worst sort of meddler—also a woman of loose morals. Of course, I was a meddling outsider, too. The note on my windshield had made that abundantly clear.

I wondered how close Jimmy had come to persona non grata in Buckeye, and hoped fervently that today's panning demonstration would be as successful as the one last week, maybe even more so. The demonstrations could bring money to town, which might mean a shift of attitude. But what if the demonstrations—and eventually the hurrah—weren't successful?

Blame would go to us meddlers. Jimmy would probably lose his job, for what it was worth. But poor Amos! He'd been branded an old fool, though he'd been more or less living with that anyway. But now he would become a pariah

in the community in which he'd spent his entire life. Us meddlers, I decided, had better succeed in what we were doing.

As Amos stepped forward to begin his presentation, I continued to study the crowd and shortly was surprised to see
Palooka O'Rourke. I hadn't noticed when he'd shown up,
but he now stood near the corner of City Hall, stolid and
stone-faced.

He was on duty; he wore a beeper attached to his belt. Was
he expecting more trouble today? The idea startled me, but
only briefly. Our "Don't tread on me" perpetrator liked to
sneak around and do his dirty work when no one was looking, which was clearly impossible with forty people looking
on. Trouble was improbable, I told myself. Palooka was just
curious. After all, he hadn't seen last week's demonstration.

Before long, I noticed, he was joined by another man. As
I watched, Palooka nodded somberly and moved his ponderous girth slightly to the side to make room for the newcomer.

The man was perhaps in his late thirties, about the same
age as Palooka. He was on the short side and none too sturdily
built. He had a surly expression, and dark greasy hair fell in
lank strands across his forehead. He wore an olive drab work-
shirt and pants, the kind sold at Sears or J. C. Penney. His
clothes were none too clean. The accumulated grime and remnants of stains gave me the impression of slipshod laundering.

I nudged Vince. "Who's that with Palooka?"

"Mike Kelly, works for Wemmer," Vince whispered. He
was watching Amos intently as he went through the routine
of burning out the gold pan.

Kelly was Wemmer's mechanic, I surmised. And Kelly, no
doubt, wasn't obliged to work on Sundays. Not officially. But
Kelly might do anything Wemmer told him to, especially if
there was a little extra money in it. Or, judging by his glowering look, he might have put the snake in the hamper or
poured oil in the Long Tom just for the hell of it.

I found myself wondering about his relationship to Palooka. Palooka who had been mighty interested in knowing
what kind of oil had been poured into the Long Tom. The

oil was dark and could well have been crankcase oil.

I stayed alert, watching the crowd, in particular Palooka and Kelly. But I could discern nothing; they were both stolid and silent.

A half-hour later Amos concluded his demonstration to loud and enthusiastic applause. His performance had benefited enormously from Trooper's coaching. She'd done an effective job of getting him to recognize when he had the audience in the palm of his hand, and also when it was time to speed up his act. With the improvement Amos had shown just since last weekend, I imagined he'd be a seasoned performer by the time of the gold country hurrah. And success was the name of the game—for all of us.

After the applause died down, Amos explained that there'd be another demonstration the following weekend. "All of you who came today," he told the crowd, "be sure to come back next Sunday—same time, same place. I'll show you how the miners used an old-time Long Tom."

There was more applause.

Amos pushed back his hat, grinning with pleasure at his success. "And I'm going to have something else," he added. "A surprise. Can't tell you what it is, but you be sure to come back. Next week, you ladies and gentlemen here today will be first in line to enjoy this surprise."

"Oooh." Frannie cooed with delight, then nudged me with her elbow. "Stagecoach," she mouthed.

I nodded my agreement.

A moment later we were startled by the blare of Hiram's car horn. Two long blasts, then two more.

"Who-eeee!" Trooper stood on the running board, waving her Aussie hat. "Who-*eeee!*"

Hiram gave another blast on the horn.

"Gather round, folks," Trooper hollered. She stood silently for a moment, hands perched at her waist, clutching her hat over one hip. "I guess you all know who I am." She paused, grinning. "Trooper Hadley's the name, far-out travel's the game."

I wondered what Trooper was up to.

"Now, as I'm sure you all know," she went on, "Buckeye is one heck of a fine town. Lots of good old-time atmosphere." She waved an arm in Amos's direction. "And, right here, we've got ourselves one first-rate old-timer. Yessir! Amos Fugaldi surely does know his oats when it comes to tellin' us about how things were done back in the mining days. Now, folks, don't you think this here demonstration Amos gave was downright fascinatin'?"

The crowd applauded again. Amos blushed.

"That's right, folks. Buckeye is a very special town, and Amos, here, is an extra-special person."

More applause.

"Well, what I'm leadin' up to is this. I'm adding another hurrah to the adventures I offer my clients, a gold country hurrah. And the most important part of this adventure will take place right here in Buckeye. Yessir, folks! Right here. And our very own Amos Fugaldi is goin' to be the star of the show. How 'bout that!"

I was astonished. We'd planned to announce the gold country hurrah later, at a press conference.

Hiram gave more blasts on the horn. Trooper threw her hat high in the air and caught it with an expert flourish. When the cheering and hoo-ha died down, Trooper began answering questions from the audience: When would the first gold country hurrah take place? What other locales would be involved? How did she plan to have her gold country adventurers travel?

After a while, someone asked how much it would cost. Trooper gave an eloquent shrug. "If you have to ask . . ." She stopped and grinned, a benevolent grin absolving from embarrassment those who might not be able to afford these expensive outings.

"Where are all these people going to stay while they're in town?" The question came from one of the locals, a man I'd seen at the Pine Cone.

"Good question," I heard another local mutter.

The riding academy offered the only local accommodations. Trooper smiled her quirky smile and put on her biggest grin. "Now, that there's a secret," she drawled.

Trooper intended to bring in tents and have people camp out, but we hadn't settled the thorny question of what land we might be able to lease. The most appropriate sites were owned by the Big Three: McCready, Truesdale, and Wemmer.

I'd thought Trooper would have been content to slide by with the easy evasion; to my surprise, she didn't let the subject go.

"But, say, you're a nice bunch of folks, so I'll go ahead and tell you the secret."

Now what?

"We'll just . . ." She'd moved into her Mae West routine, moving one shoulder suggestively and patting an imaginary blond hairdo. "Ah . . . we'll just have everybody come on up to my place."

Someone in the crowd giggled nervously.

I smelled trouble. Outrageous answers were something I'd come to recognize as a signal Trooper was skating on thin ice—just like the grin or the drawl.

I checked for audience reactions. Some of the Sunday tourists seemed mildly amused, but not the townspeople. I glanced over toward City Hall, expecting to see Palooka as impassive as ever and Kelly still glowering. But only Palooka was there.

$\triangledown$

# 16

FRANNIE INVITED TROOPER and Vince to join us for supper that night. "Gracious!" she said as she put a pottery casserole filled to the brim with enchiladas in the center of the table. "I've had the heebie-jeebies all day, ever since somebody put oil in the Long Tom thing."

Heebie-jeebies. It was as good a way as any other, I thought, to describe my uneasy feelings, particularly about Trooper's odd use of her Mae West routine, which no one else had commented on.

"But all's well that ends well," Frannie went on. "The rest of the day, everything happened just perfectly, don't you think?"

"Jeez," Vince said. "I kept thinking something else was gonna go wrong. But the whole thing, what Amos did, went smooth as mashed potatoes."

"Absolutely," Trooper concurred. But her enthusiasm was mechanical. I watched with more than passing interest as she dawdled over small portions of enchilada and salad.

"For heaven's sake," Frannie said. "That's scarcely enough to feed a bird. Take some more, Trooper. And don't you want some sour cream or guacamole? There's extra olives, too."

Trooper refused in a small, weary voice. Her fatigue sounded authentic, but it was out of character—at odds with the boundless energy she seemed to have on earlier occasions. That strange come-and-go limp was back, too.

Her behavior was an enigma. I was increasingly uneasy

about the half-cocked response she'd made to the man who
wanted to know where the hurrah participants would stay.
I would have expected her to gloss over the question as
quickly as possible. The Mae West bit only served to focus
attention on the issue. And on the ride home, she'd been
silent; when we'd gotten back to Frannie's she went upstairs
to take a nap.

She *was* genuinely tired. Still, I couldn't shake the suspi-
cion she also was using her fatigue to avoid us.

Trooper had spent a great deal of time in private conversations with Jimmy while we were in Buckeye. Come to
think of it, she'd spent nearly all her free time with him,
except for her stint coaching Amos. They were going over
the publicity plans, I told myself at first. But she and Jimmy,
having spent over an hour together before the demonstration, had another hour-long session afterward. Even more
curious, Jimmy had become suddenly secretive—self-con-
scious, wary of carrying on even a minor conversation with
Vince or me. Or even Frannie. If I hadn't liked him so much,
I could have sworn he was behaving as if he were guilty. But
of what?

"Emma," Frannie said sharply. "What in the world are
you thinking about? I've asked you twice—would you like
another enchilada?"

"Sorry, Frannie. Yes, thanks, I would."

I accepted a second portion of enchilada, heaped with
guacamole, sour cream, and olives. Frannie gave second portions to Vince and served her own plate, too. "So," she said.
"What's on tap for tomorrow?"

"Nothing much for me," Vince replied. "I got to stay in
Fairville and work the day shift for a buddy. His wife's in the
hospital."

"Oh, my," Frannie said. "I hope it's nothing serious."

"Naw. She's gonna have a baby. They set the date last
week—you know, the operation where they take the baby
out of the mother."

Frannie turned to me with an inquiring look.

"I'll be working, too. Tomorrow's the day I have to do that job—clear out Portuguese Hall."

I figured I could make short work of it and be in Buckeye by early afternoon, but I didn't want Frannie to know that. Or Vince either.

"How about you? What are you going to do tomorrow?" Frannie asked Trooper.

"I'm going out to Buckeye to explore that back road into town, the one Amos said was the stagecoach route in the old days. I hope to use it to bring the hurrah participants into town. By stagecoach, of course."

"Oooh, how fascinating." Frannie spoke a little too brightly. She was dying to go along, it was obvious.

"I think it'll be a pretty rugged trip," Trooper said. "I want to go alone. I may have to do some hiking to check out possible trouble spots along the route."

Frannie's expectant smile froze in place. A rugged trip. Hiking. The expedition wouldn't include her.

I felt sympathy for Frannie. Trooper needn't have thrown in the bit about hiking. And I was a little surprised she was planning the excursion for tomorrow—not that she planned to check the route, but that she decided to do it so soon. It could have been a hasty decision, made after both Vince and I declared plans to be elsewhere. But then, she must have some reason for wanting to make the trip alone, or could it be her plans included Jimmy and she didn't want us to know?

"Um," Trooper said, more a throat-clearing sound than an actual word. The quirky, one-sided smile made a brief appearance, then just as quickly was suppressed. "Being as neither Emma nor Vince is going out to Buckeye tomorrow, I suppose I'll need to rent a car."

"Oh, no need!" Frannie's fixed smile remained in place. "I'll be happy to lend you mine." The smile faded. "I'm not going anywhere tomorrow."

"Why, I do thank you kindly."

An awkward silence followed. Seeking to change the subject, I turned to Trooper. "You told us you had a Mexican trip scheduled before we do our hurrah," I said. "I'd like very much to hear what it will be like."

I'd saved the day. Frannie looked up, smiling. "Heavens," she said, the cheery hostess again. "You must have lots of exciting things planned. Tell us about it."

"We start at San Blas, the old harbor on the west coast of Mexico," Trooper said. "During colonial days it was one of the most important ports on the Pacific routes. But now it's a forgotten city, bypassed by time." She continued, travelog style, talking about the splendors of stone ruins to be seen in the jungle, quaint houses and tropical flowers, the un-spoiled coastline.

Frannie settled back happily, her equilibrium restored, while Trooper slid into spinning yarns about eccentric clients and unexpected events on some of the previous Mexican trips, as well as her favorite conservation projects—pristine beaches saved from development, tropical forests kept safe from logging, bays and wetlands reclaimed.

By now Trooper's fatigue seemed to have vanished; she was altogether her old self. And later, after Vince had left and Frannie had refused our help in the kitchen, she and I got to talking about what we had in common as operators of one-woman businesses. We had a good time at it; I'm always happy to engage in a getting-to-know-you session with an-other woman. But our conversation ended suddenly when I asked how she had managed to put together the capital to launch her first hurrah.

Trooper stood up, quite abruptly. "Shucks, sweetie," she said, switching to all-out drawl. "I did it flat on my back, workin' as a hooker."

She turned on her heel, stalked out of the room, and stomped up the stairs. I was left with absolutely no idea whether this was the truth or one of her spur-of-the-moment conversation stoppers.

▽

# 17

I THOUGHT ABOUT Trooper all morning as I cleaned out Portuguese Hall. Erratic was the word to describe her recent behavior, I decided. And it was a marked change from her behavior at Amos's first gold panning demonstration and during her first stay at Frannie's. She'd been outrageous at times. Downright flaky. But back then, only a week ago, her every act—everything she said or did—was geared to furthering her purposes. Even the off-the-wall statements she'd made last week had served some use, most often to end a conversation. She'd seemed a tireless, smoothly oiled machine, with no wasted motion and a useful outcome for every bit of effort.

Her wild-card remarks yesterday had me stumped. Well, maybe she'd wanted to end our conversation when she threw in that business about being a hooker. But the Mae West routine she'd pulled in Buckeye made absolutely no sense. Nor did her surprise announcement of the gold country hurrah.

I finished clearing out Portuguese Hall by noon, and turned my mind to the puzzle of Sam Jones. I had no idea why he let me bid the contract so high; realtors were usually sharp-cookie employers. I shrugged off my curiosity. Maybe he'd never done that sort of work; the assignments I take on can look formidable to people who've never had to get their hands dirty. At any rate, I wasn't going to turn over the keys until tomorrow afternoon, keeping up the pretense that the job took two days.

With the work at Portuguese Hall taken care of, I headed

immediately for Buckeye and Marie's Doughnut Shop. One of Aggie's hamburgers would go just right—better yet, I might be able to pick up some gossip.

Aggie was at her usual post, a grease-stained apron tied around her thick middle. I gave my order for a burger and coffee, all the while aware of a steady stare from those pale eyes in that pale face. Aggie slapped a hamburger pattie on the grill and began her ministrations with the spatula, scraping away grease and from time to time pressing down on the meat.

She finally spoke. "Your fancy friend has been all over town this morning." Her lips were compressed in a thin line. Disapproval.

"My friend?"

She glared at me. "Damn right! Your friend—that Hadley female." She gave a final push on the meat with her spatula, mercilessly squeezing out the juice, and turned to prepare the paper plate with its portion of lettuce and tomato and bag of potato chips. "She's been parading her fanny in them funny pants, getting everybody stirred up."

Everybody? What did Aggie mean?

"Damn shame she encouraged Amos in the first place. Old Amos ought to know better, making a fool of himself with them panning demonstrations." She plunked the hamburger down at my place, then looked me square in the eye. "You know what I'm talking about. You was there yesterday. Just like you was that first time, too." She turned her back and busied herself cleaning the grill. No chance I'd learn more from her. Her impassive back sent a clear message: I was part of the enemy camp.

I took my hamburger to a table in the corner and sat facing outward toward the parking area. If Trooper was in Buckeye, I thought, I might see her pass by—there'd be no mistaking Frannie's Mercedes. Or maybe she was already checking out the old stagecoach route. No, she wouldn't do that in Frannie's car. Maybe she'd arranged for Amos to take her. I'd have to check at his house later.

A police car pulled into the parking area. Palooka heaved

himself out of it, then approached, greeting me with a curt nod, and opened the door of the doughnut shop with ponderous care. He moved toward the counter.

"The usual?" Aggie asked, favoring him with one of her grins. He nodded.

She loaded a half-dozen doughnuts into a paper bag, then added one extra and a handful of paper napkins, after which she withdrew an oversize mug from under the counter and filled it with coffee. "Put it on the tab?"

"Yes, thanks."

Ignoring me, he went to one of the farthest-away picnic tables and settled down to begin working his way through the doughnuts. I sat, munching on my hamburger—dry, thanks to Aggie's anger—and absentmindedly studied the miscellaneous collection of small houses on the slope beyond. The king-of-the-hill house that belonged to Truesdale with its failed pretentiousness and mismatched collection of trim styles was certainly unappealing—most inappropriate for the pastels-and-pearls Mrs. Truesdale.

A ratty-looking Nissan pickup pulled into the parking area and stopped beside the patrol car. Mike Kelly. He came inside, got a cup of coffee, and went back out to join Palooka, all without so much as a glance at me.

I watched the two of them, fascinated. They had their backs to me, so I couldn't see their faces. Kelly was going on about something to Palooka, complete with vociferous, denunciatory gestures; Palooka sat as unmoving as a rock. Maybe I could make a chance to catch the drift of their conversation.

I went inside and put money for the hamburger and a respectable tip on the counter. Aggie, making a show of cleaning the grill, didn't look up. I went back out and approached Palooka and Kelly as quietly as I could.

"Damn bitch! Bad enough we got—" Kelly broke off, suddenly aware of my presence.

I looked at the two men, briefly, as I walked past. Palooka's expression was neutral. Kelly glared sullenly back at me. I assumed when I heard him speak he'd been talking about Trooper. But he could have been talking about me.

I walked on more quickly, got in my truck, and headed on up Buckeye Boulevard.

I drove slowly through the old downtown, looking for Frannie's Mercedes. I didn't see it, but instead spotted Jimmy entering the *Bugle* office. I hurried to park the truck and find out what I could from him.

Inside the newspaper office, Jimmy stood behind the service counter, a rather bemused look on his face. I asked if he'd seen Trooper. He motioned that I should come into his office, and then closed the door. "I was just with her. We had a planning session at my home."

"You two sure have been doing a lot of planning."

"There's a lot to plan for." He smiled, gazing off into space.

There was no point in pussyfooting around. "Like what?" I said. "What's to spend so much time planning for, just the two of you?"

Jimmy turned back to me, still smiling. "Sit down," he said. "This is going to take a while."

I sat in the rickety wooden office chair he indicated.

"Trooper didn't want me to tell you yesterday, or anyone. But this morning she said it was all right."

"Tell what?" I said, exasperated.

Jimmy leaned back. "You know Trooper's been into conservation. She's set up foundations to protect wildlife and natural resources—historic preservation, too, that sort of thing."

I nodded, impatient for him to get on with it.

"Well, that's exactly what she's going to do here. She's talked to her lawyers in Los Angeles and worked out the details already. She says most of the paperwork's done, too." He leaned forward eagerly. "There's going to be a Buckeye Foundation to preserve open space and historic sites. And there's more. For one thing, you just happen to be looking at the new executive director of said Buckeye Foundation."

I was surprised—also relieved to have an explanation for the long sessions between Jimmy and Trooper.

"Congratulations," I said.

"There's more."

"More?"

"That's right. All of Trooper's other foundations are to be rolled into this one, the Buckeye Foundation." He leaned back, beaming with pride. "And I'm going to be in charge of the whole thing. She told me that just this morning." He folded his arms across his chest with satisfaction. "I have a new job."

I was stunned. The whole thing was all out of proportion. And sudden. Far too sudden.

"Where's Trooper?" I asked.

"She's over in Leona, seeing a lawyer about getting power of attorney for me. She's anxious to have the details off her back. She'll sign the power of attorney on the spot and the lawyer will mail it directly to me." Jimmy leaned back in his chair, his eyes bright and preternaturally large behind his thick-lensed glasses.

Why was Trooper pushing things so fast? Jimmy was eager and dedicated, but he couldn't know much about running a foundation—certainly not an entire group of foundations. It made no sense for Trooper to put the whole ball of wax in his hands. I began formulating questions to ask Jimmy. And Trooper.

He interrupted my thoughts. "Piccard was in here first thing this morning, before Trooper told me I'd head the other foundations, too. He told me not to run a story on the sabotage to the Long Tom, and he didn't want the story about Amos to be any more than a short item." He lowered his head, smiling in the way that reminded me of his mother. "Next time Piccard comes in . . ." He enunciated his words slowly, giving great emphasis to each. "Next time . . . he's going to find out he's lost himself an editor-boy."

I thought for a moment. "Your job with this new Buckeye Foundation starts immediately?"

"Im-*me*-diately!"

"So who's going to put together the newspaper this week?"

Jimmy shrugged. "I've got better things to do."

"Such as put together the foundation?"

"Exactly. Plus I've got some other research I plan to do."

"What research is that?"

"Something I've already been working on, an investigation of McCready and his investments."

"Not Truesdale and Wemmer?"

"Nope. The deal McCready has put together with them is only the tip of the iceberg, only one part of the McCready investment empire. He's just using them to help put through the annexation. Mr. Big is keeping real quiet about it, but along with the land he and his partners plan to develop, the annexation also includes a big chunk that still belongs to Consolidated. It's the land east of town."

I worked to catch up with what Jimmy was telling me.

"So," I said finally. "McCready may be long retired from Consolidated, but he's still Consolidated's man."

"And for good reason." Jimmy leaned forward, his expression taking on an angry cast. "There's a huge profit to be made, both for McCready and Consolidated. Here's how it works. First, McCready paves the way for the annexation, which is a deal he's been planning for years. He's waited until the time was just right. Now. And he's just gotten confirmation of some very important news."

"What's that?"

"The Tengold Community College District has hush-hush plans for future expansion. It's absolutely definite, their new campus is slated for that hilly land east of town. And McCready is going to get rewarded big time for his loyalty." He leaned forward, eager to confide. "As soon as the land is annexed, Consolidated sells a chunk of it to the college district for the new campus, making a fat profit. Then Consolidated gives McCready a good deal—deferred payments, I don't know what—so he can buy an adjoining, major-size piece of real estate. It's choice: rolling hills, plenty of oak trees, a good view. About then, McCready will probably retire from city government. And his new chunk of land becomes an upscale subdivision adjoining the campus."

"Whew!" I said. "McCready's got more reason than anybody to want the annexation to go through."

"That's right. Wemmer and Truesdale are just . . . conveniences."

I sat back, still trying to wrap my mind around this new revelation. I felt suddenly apprehensive about Jimmy's safety, considering the information he was digging up. McCready could be dangerous in never-to-be-found-out ways, I had no doubt of that.

"You've got proof of all this you've told me?" I asked.

"I'm working on it. I was going to sell the story. It'll be a humdinger."

"Who'll run it?" Not the *Bugle*, obviously.

"There's always the highest bidder," Jimmy said confidently. "Only now, maybe I'll make it a foundation project." He clasped his hands behind his head and regarded me expectantly. The situation called for me to say something laudatory, but I had too many concerns about the wisdom of the project. I could come up with nothing.

I was saved by the unexpected arrival of Hiram Cohen. He knocked lightly on the office door and at the same time opened it and poked his head in.

"Have you seen Trooper?" he asked anxiously.

It seemed she'd phoned Hiram last night and made arrangements to have lunch with him today.

"I supposed she meant at that New Pine Cone place. I waited and waited and she never showed up."

"She's over in Leona getting some legal papers drawn up," Jimmy volunteered. "I thought she'd be back by now, but it probably took longer than she expected."

"You think so?" Hiram looked hopeful.

"Are you sure she meant to meet you at the Pine Cone?" I asked.

Hiram shrugged. "I suppose."

"Well, there is one other restaurant in town," I said. "Why don't you let me show you where it is? Maybe she'll be there."

That Trooper should be at the Yellow Lantern was altogether improbable. But I welcomed the excuse to get away from Jimmy long enough to put some serious thought to everything he'd told me, and what to say to him about it. Or to his mother.

Hiram had his Lincoln parked by the curb. He glanced at my truck, parked down the street. "Can we take my car? I hate to leave her unattended for any length of time."

"Fine with me," I said.

Within moments we were rolling down Buckeye's main street. Hiram had the top down; I took pleasure in the ride as we moved majestically along.

"Trooper is driving Frannie's car," I said. "It's a Mercedes. We ought to be able to spot her the minute she's back in town."

"I certainly hope so."

I directed him to follow Buckeye Boulevard to its eastern intersection with Highway 18. There was no Mercedes parked in the Yellow Lantern lot—no surprise.

"Turn right," I said. "We can go back along Highway 18." Maybe Trooper would be at the Fugaldi place, assuming she was back from Leona. She must have forgotten about her date with Hiram, which was one more item to add to the list of puzzling things she'd done lately.

I spotted Frannie's Mercedes moments later, as we passed Wemmer's sales lot.

"Pull over to the side," I requested.

Hiram fussed about pulling off onto the shoulder, rolling along until he found a place he deemed suitably wide and firm. He wanted to get all four wheels off the pavement without danger of scratches from the roadside brush.

Long before he'd gotten us parked, I'd turned around in my seat, trying to keep my eyes locked on the Mercedes to make sure Trooper wasn't leaving.

"What do you suppose she's doing there?" Hiram asked.

"Beats me."

I tried to think. Wemmer's agency, of all places. Why *would* she be there?

# 18

We sat in Hiram's Lincoln, watching and waiting. Trooper's reason for being at Wemmer's agency soon became apparent. She and a salesman emerged from the sales hut, engrossed in conversation, and went over to a little four-wheel-drive vehicle. Trooper walked around it, studying it briefly. It was a Geo—a slick little thing, quite tiny. And with no top, only a roll bar.

"I know what she's doing," I said. "She's renting the Geo to check out the old stagecoach road."

"Do you think she's forgotten about our lunch?" Hiram asked plaintively.

I felt like telling him to draw his own conclusions but instead kept silent. And kept my eye on Wemmer's sales lot. Moments later Trooper and the salesman went back inside. Then Mike Kelly emerged from the repair bay, hopped into the Geo, and drove it inside, out of sight. I wondered what he was doing; the possibilities made me nervous.

"Both Wemmer and his mechanic—the man who just took that vehicle into the service bay—are opposed to Trooper's gold country hurrah," I told Hiram. "Vehemently opposed."

Hiram looked at me blankly through his rimless glasses. "Surely, Mr. Wemmer or the other man wouldn't . . ."

I twisted in the seat. "Lord! I wish I could see what Kelly's doing."

Hiram handed me a large, old-fashioned pair of binoculars. "Here. Would these help?"

I doubted it, but took them anyway. After a moment's fussing with the adjustment, I could see the area around the service bay in detail, even to the prices on the gas pumps. But it was too dark to see inside.

"Drat!" I muttered, lowering the glasses.

We waited. At last, Trooper came out of the sales hut carrying a sheaf of papers, the salesman following. Shortly after, Kelly brought the Geo from the repair bay. I raised the glasses again. The salesman opened the door for Trooper to get in and spent a few moments showing her how to operate it. Not until Trooper bent forward to turn on the ignition did it come to mind that she'd be heading east on Highway 18.

"Hiram, she'll be going toward the mountains. We've got to stop her."

He looked at me—again the blank stare.

"She's going up the old stagecoach road, with a lot of steep switchbacks. That little Geo may have been sabotaged. You've got to get this car turned around. We'll catch up and stop her."

He still didn't seem to get it.

"The brakes could be fixed to go out," I said, almost shouting. "Or maybe the steering. You don't understand how some people in this town feel about Trooper."

"Well, if you really think . . ." Hiram looked unconvinced, but started the Lincoln and began the laborious process of turning it around on the narrow highway.

By this time Trooper had gotten into the Geo. She turned it in a tight circle, and, with a wave to the salesman, headed out of the sales lot and turned east on Highway 18. By the time Hiram had the Lincoln turned around, she had quite a lead on us; we lost sight of her around a curve.

The stagecoach road, according to Amos, veered sharply off to the left about two miles east of Buckeye. I spotted it easily. "Turn here," I said.

Hiram made the turn with last-minute clumsiness, then braked to a stop. The fresh tracks of the Geo were clearly visible in the soft earth of the old road, as was the route as it zigzagged up the steep ridge ahead.

At the top, Amos had said, the old road joined Highway 49, the main north-south route through the Mother Lode country. I gazed upward, letting my eyes follow its path. Sometimes it was easily seen, sometimes hidden behind overgrowth. At the top of the ridge springtime clouds edged the sky, standing out white and fluffy against the clear, deep blue.

The road would easily be passable for Trooper. But the Lincoln was much longer, twice the Geo's wheelbase length. We'd have a time getting around the switchbacks. Hiram stared ahead disconsolately. The road was narrow; bushes and small trees crowded it on both sides.

I put a hand on his arm. "I know. But I'm afraid Trooper is going to need our help."

He said nothing.

"Think! What if the steering went out and she went over the side?"

Hiram groaned.

"There are some mighty steep hillsides up there."

He resolutely shifted gears and started forward.

Things weren't too bad at first. We moved up a gentle slope, bushes scraping the sides of the car only now and then. Each occasion, however, evoked a wince from Hiram.

I imagined we were gaining on Trooper, and told him so, hoping to encourage him to keep up a speedy pace. "The sooner we catch her," I urged, "the less damage to your car." He gave me a look of dire distress, but said nothing.

As we approached the face of the ridge and the first of the switchbacks, I spotted Trooper's vehicle rounding the turn at the far end.

"There she is! Use your horn."

Hiram honked the horn repeatedly. Trooper should have been able to hear it, but she didn't stop.

"What's *with* her?" I muttered.

Hiram sped uphill toward the first switchback turn, braking only at the last moment. He cranked hard on the wheel, trying to get the big car as far as possible around the uphill curve of the road, but couldn't make it on one try. He shifted into reverse, sweat breaking out on his forehead, then backed slowly, at the same time pulling with all his might to get the wheel cranked in the other direction.

"Let me help," I said. I hopped out and went to see how near the back wheels were to the edge, urging him backward. "Stop!" I hollered at the last minute, and hurried to get back into the car.

He shifted gears, and then, as he edged the car forward, pulled furiously on the wheel. It was close. A front fender scraped noisily against the embankment. Hiram, sweating and working hard, managed to turn the wheel another little bit. I closed my eyes, as if by not witnessing it I somehow could escape knowledge of Hiram's misery over what was happening to his beautiful car.

At the next switchback, and the one after that, we repeated the process. Hiram would turn as much as he could on the first try, then I'd hop out and check how far he could back up safely. On the uphill straightaways I scanned the road ahead. I could spot Trooper only when she crossed an open space where my view was not obscured. Finally, when I could see that she was a full three switchback turns ahead of us, I gave up the notion of catching her.

I laid a hand on Hiram's arm and pointed to the mountainside above. "There's three switchback turns between us now." I didn't want to quit. "I guess it's no use," I said reluctantly.

Hiram shook his head. "We have to go to the top. I can't turn around. Just hope the tires hold out."

The next switchback was steep and tricky. We took our time. By now the afternoon had turned cool; a stiff upcanyon wind was blowing. The fluffy white ridgetop clouds had transformed themselves; they were now thunderheads, dark and foreboding.

We continued. The car began to overheat; occasional wisps of steam wreathed the hood ornament. But Hiram didn't seem worried. In fact, he seemed to be pushing the car faster than ever on the straightaways.

I could still see Trooper when her car was out in the open. Then the Geo, which had been bumping speedily uphill, abruptly stopped.

"Hiram! Look! What do you suppose she's doing now?"

I used the binoculars. Trooper was out of the vehicle and stood beside it, fishing for something in her purse. I couldn't be sure what she drew out, but it must have been a pocket-knife, because moments later she began cutting long branches of the mountain redbud that grew profusely by the side of the road.

"She's cutting flowers!"

Hiram gripped the wheel. "Maybe we'll catch her yet."

We pushed forward again, Hiram by this time completely heedless of the branches slapping the side of his car. At the next switchback he downshifted but didn't drop speed as much as on previous turns. He hauled mightily on the steering wheel; the rear of the car slewed in the loose gravel and we made the turn without having to stop.

"Attaboy!" I shouted.

Trooper continued to pick redbud branches, apparently intent on amassing a huge armful.

Another switchback—this time I again had to get out and direct Hiram through the backup process. By now the wind had increased. Trees bent in the mountain gale; the wind made a rushing sound. I shivered.

Trooper was out of sight for a while, but I had a clear view of the ridgetop. Clouds billowed ominously; the dark sky threatened. I looked for lightning, inevitable with a spring thunderstorm, but didn't see any.

The next switchback was worse than any we'd encountered so far. I again had to direct Hiram, standing wind-whipped, shouting to be heard above the storm.

As soon as we started again I saw Trooper.

"She's still stopped," I yelled to Hiram, "but she's getting back into the Geo." I tried for a closer look with the binoculars—no easy task with the jouncing and lurching of Hiram's car on the rough road. Trooper had heaped her bundle of redbud branches on the seat beside her, but I had no idea what she wanted with them. I'd have thought her too efficient to pick flowers for mere enjoyment.

Trooper, now back in the driver's seat, sat rigid for a moment. Then she leaned forward to start the ignition.

"Hurry! She's going to go on!"

Hiram nodded, his hands clenching the wheel, his mouth a grim line. The lightning began quite suddenly: sharp cracks, blinding flashes of light with thunder following immediately. I struggled to keep the binoculars on Trooper, getting a clear view from time to time despite the jouncing. I had the impression of seeing a scene illuminated by strobes. The lightning flashes afforded brief images of Trooper. She sat stiffly erect, her hands on the wheel, the roll bar behind her head.

One particularly strong flash of light gave me a clear image. Trooper's hands moved on the Geo's steering wheel as she began to crank it around slowly for the next turn. She jerked violently—could it be she was frightened of lightning? An instant later I lost the strobe-picture image. Frustrated, I set aside the binoculars.

Hiram and I watched the Geo. It lurched toward the edge of the embankment, then slowed and almost stopped. It lurched again, teetered on the edge, and then hung endlessly, two wheels out over thin air. Slowly, inevitably, it tilted forward. As we watched helplessly, it went over.

The Lincoln came to a lurching stop. Hiram turned off the engine and sat motionless, his face white. Wind, loud and terrible, swooshed through the trees. Lightning struck all around, the rolls of thunder deafening.

My mind flooded with imagination-created images of the downward course of the Geo. I saw the descent in strobe-picture images, the little vehicle bouncing, lurching ever downward, plunging into the steep canyon.

"Dear Lord!"

Hiram stared at me.

"Start the car again," I urged.

He turned on the ignition, downshifted; we moved slowly forward.

We had one last switchback to negotiate. Hiram, as if in a trance, shifted gears and turned the wheel. By the time we reached the spot where Trooper had gone off the road the lightning strikes had begun to abate. Moments later the storm's first raindrops splattered to the ground.

We climbed out of the car, slowly, stood staring in horror at the spot where Trooper's little Geo had gone over the edge. Suddenly, without warning, Hiram gave an incoherent yell. He started running. At the edge of the road, without even a glance at the abyss below, he started downward.

"Don't!" I dashed forward.

I got to him just as he lost his footing. He was on his back, feet flailing, beginning a downward slide in the slippery shale. I dropped to my knees. "Give me your hand!" I grabbed, catching him. I'd stopped his momentum, but his feet were out from under him. I doubted I'd be able to hang on long.

"Turn over," I yelled, "get on your hands and knees." Hiram, eyes bulging now that he was aware of the danger, scrambled energetically. I pulled on his hand, using my other hand to cling to a small tree. Moments later I'd hauled him back. We huddled on the rain-splotched soil of the dusty embankment, momentarily too spent to say anything.

After a while I scrambled to my feet, then offered a hand to Hiram. "There's nothing you could have done to help Trooper," I said. He nodded numbly, then got to his feet. Together we moved toward the edge of the road and looked over.

The Geo must have descended into the canyon very much as I had imagined; it had left behind a trail of torn brush and broken tree limbs. I caught my breath. At intervals in the downward path were clumps of redbud branches, their color barely discernible in the dwindling light.

# 19

Hiram and I continued the short distance up the old road to the top of the ridge and Highway 49. Until then, we'd been unmindful of the pelting rain; now it seemed that being back on a well-traveled highway had somehow returned us to the realities of the everyday world. Hiram stopped, put up the top, then produced an old-fashioned car robe; we spread it across our backs and hugged it around our shoulders. Shivering, we drove south, then turned west on Highway 18 for the twenty-minute ride back to Buckeye.

Palooka was on duty at the police department. He phoned a report to the sheriff's emergency crew—also McCready—immediately afterward.

McCready interrogated us on the details of the accident, apparently in his capacity as city manager. I resented his bland air of neutrality, as if his interest were purely a matter of official duty. Hypocrite! He knew full well we were aligned with Trooper and against his development scheme.

After we'd each given our initial statements, McCready grilled us—very courteously—about the afternoon's events. "Do you know why Mrs. Hadley came to Buckeye today? Why would she drive up that disused road? Do you suppose she knew it was dangerous? You say she stopped to pick redbud in bloom—can you offer any explanation for this behavior? Why would an outdoorswoman as experienced as Mrs. Hadley lose control of her vehicle?"

Then came the sticky one.

"Just exactly why did you two feel it was necessary to

follow Mrs. Hadley and attempt to overtake her?"

There was no way I would have answered that last question truthfully. It came from the man who might have arranged Trooper's death, or at least was in league with whoever was responsible for her death. I suggested, inanely, that Hiram and I were worried about Trooper being alone on the mountainside with a storm coming up, at which Hiram regarded me strangely but nodded as if in agreement. I thanked my lucky stars that McCready hadn't chosen to interview us separately.

While McCready was questioning us, Palooka was busy on the phone with the sheriff's men in Leona. I caught scraps of their conversation about map quadrants, tow trucks, and who might have winch equipment capable of pulling the Geo back up from the canyon. Before long, Palooka's dinner-hour replacement arrived, and he interrupted McCready's questioning to give him a brief report, saying there was no hope of retrieving the vehicle before morning. "I'm going out for my dinner hour, Mr. McCready," he concluded.

I watched Palooka's bulky form disappear out the door into the gathering twilight, certain he was headed for Marie's Doughnut Shop. The whole town would soon learn what had happened, or at least Aggie's interpretation of what Palooka told her. No doubt she'd offer plenty of conjecture, all of it putting Trooper in the worst light.

McCready, throughout his questioning, had maintained a scrupulous politeness. Now he began making farewells with equal courtesy.

"Thank you very much, Mrs. Chizzit and Mr. Cohen, for your cooperation. I apologize for detaining you at such an unhappy time, but I am sure you understand the necessity. Perhaps you will be good enough to stay in contact during the investigation of this unfortunate incident. But we'll have no further information until the sheriff's crews bring the vehicle and . . . ah . . . when they bring everything up from the canyon. That will be tomorrow afternoon, at the soonest."

Without saying a word I took hold of Hiram's arm and steered him out the door. Hiram took me back to my truck. I was dead tired, but I still had an hour's drive back to Sacramento.

By the time I pulled into Frannie's driveway I wanted nothing more than to be alone and take a hot shower. No questions. No explanations. Just sleep. But there was Frannie to be considered. She was waiting for me; her kitchen light was still on. I put the truck into the garage, glanced yearningly at the stairway to my apartment, and then went over to knock on Frannie's porch door.

"Come on in, Emma."

I let myself in and proceeded to the kitchen. Frannie was sitting in her breakfast nook. In the sink was an empty ice cream dish—Frannie always eats ice cream when she's upset.

"Jimmy called with the news," she said. "Gracious! This is just terrible!" She wiped her eyes with a damp tissue.

I sat down beside her and took her hand.

"Oh, do you want some ice cream? There's plenty."

"No, thanks."

"What happened? All Jimmy knew was that Trooper went off the road . . . and . . . she's dead. Oh—he wants to talk to you. Tomorrow, I guess. But do you really think the accident was . . . ? Is she really dead?"

I remembered my last clear view of Trooper through the binoculars—her erect posture, the stiff set of her shoulders. And the roll bar crossing behind her head, no other protection. I saw again the Geo teetering at the edge of the switchback, the trail of torn brush and tree limbs that marked the violence of its pathway down the steep canyon.

"She's dead. There's no doubt."

Frannie put both elbows on the table and cupped her chin in her hands. "Tell me the way everything happened."

When I'd told my story Frannie was silent for a long while. "I've been thinking about Trooper all evening," she said at last. "She acted *so* strangely, I mean ever since she came back from Los Angeles."

"I thought so, too. And I can't get over how she stopped to pick redbud."

"She picked flowers?"

"She cut a great armload of redbud. She had them on the seat beside her when . . . when she went over."

Frannie was silent for another long moment, then turned to me, her brown eyes luminous with tears. "Do you know what I think?"

I shook my head, not trusting myself to speak.

"Trooper killed herself. Something was wrong, that's why she started acting so strangely. Something was terribly wrong that she couldn't do anything about, and so she killed herself."

"You might well be right."

"I know I'm right," Frannie said mournfully. "That's why she picked the flowers. To die with."

Later, thinking things over before I went to sleep, I realized the suicide idea didn't cover everything. Trooper might indeed have gone up the old road intending to kill herself, but she'd been given an assist. In one flash of light I'd seen her hands on the steering wheel as she started to make the turn; an instant later, in the next flash, I'd seen her jerk strangely. Only then had the Geo faltered and at last gone over the edge. The point was, she'd started the turn. There was no reason for her to start a turn she didn't intend to complete.

She could have been shot. We wouldn't have heard, not over the sounds of the storm. The killer could have taken the quick way to the ridgetop—east on Highway 18 and north on 49—then hiked the short distance to a position within range of that last switchback.

All of this, of course, assumed the killer knew Trooper had gone up that old road.

$\triangledown$

# 20

IN THE DAYS following Trooper's death I was more and more
aware of an enormous sense of loss. I found myself scarcely
believing that I had known her only a week. The same
seemed to hold true for Jimmy and Amos. Frannie, too. Even
Vince was affected.

Jimmy had the worst of it. His college kid attitude had
vanished; no trace remained of either his wry sense of humor
or his easygoing ways. On Tuesday, Jimmy had handed over
to Oliver Piccard his letter of resignation, an event he'd earlier contemplated with gleeful anticipation but which now
held no satisfaction for him.

He labored early and late to carry out Trooper's wishes for
the Buckeye Foundation. Grim with determination, he wondered constantly what she'd meant by this or that and ago-
nized over every decision. I talked with Jimmy often, hoping
I might be useful as a sounding board. For one thing,
Trooper's death did not attract immediate attention despite
her worldwide reputation. She'd rented the Geo as Mary Jane
Hadley. That was the name that went on the sheriff's reports
and also on the autopsy and inquest schedule. It attracted no
attention from reporters; Jimmy and I were content with that.

"I want to notify her next of kin and don't know yet who
they are," Jimmy said. "Besides, I need the time—a week or
so if I can get it—to contact all the places where she set up
foundations." He looked up at me with a wan smile.
"Trooper would want the most publicity possible out of this.
I think we'll do simultaneous memorial services."

"And also in keeping with Trooper's style, wring every possible bit of fund-raising out of this?"

"You got it." And it was back, the wry grin.

I breathed an inward sigh of relief. I'd been worried about Jimmy, and was at a loss about what to tell his mother. But now I was sure he was going to land on his feet, at least emotionally, which is what counts.

There were plenty more decisions to be made: how to run the Buckeye Foundation, for instance, and how to get the hurrah moving. Jimmy was determined to carry this through according to Trooper's wishes. We'd all agreed to help and declared ourselves Jimmy's team: me, Amos, Frannie, Vince, and Hiram. Before Trooper's death we'd been excited at the prospect of a gold country hurrah and wondered what she'd do to carry it off. Now we knew it was up to us to make it succeed.

On Wednesday afternoon Jimmy had a phone call from the lawyer in Leona who'd made up the power of attorney for Trooper, and learned she also had made a new will and named him executor. I was as astonished as he. Why had Trooper heaped the additional load on him? Surely she had relatives who would have been more appropriate as executor.

Or did she?

I'd had no hint from her that she had a personal life separate from the hurrahs. Still, people had mothers and fathers. Siblings. Cousins. Surely Trooper had relatives, even if she was on the outs with them. In any event, we'd know more by early next week—Jimmy had asked me to go to Los Angeles and check out her apartment.

Meanwhile, Vince proved to be a major help. The first thing, he'd checked Kelly's alibi for the afternoon of Trooper's death. Wemmer's mechanic hadn't gone anywhere; in fact, he had worked an hour overtime.

"We got more of a slippery case with McCready and the other two. McCready was out and about, supposedly working. Ditto for Wemmer and Truesdale, but so far I ain't found nobody that seen 'em."

Bulldog Valenti also reported that he'd driven up to the spot where the old stagecoach road joined Highway 49 to do a little investigating of his own.

"The sheriff's guys were up there looking, too," he told me. "But they wasn't giving it the going over I was. I marked that hillside off into a grid, searched every bit of it that was level enough to stand on. I found two sets of shell casings. My guess is one of them was left by someone shooting at Trooper."

I mentally thanked Vince for his stubbornness, no matter how often I'd complained about it.

"The sheriff's office didn't want to hear about the shell casings; they said casings was all over these hillsides. But I told them they'd feel different as soon as they done an autopsy and found bullets in her."

Which was exactly what happened.

On Thursday, after the autopsy report was in, the sheriff's men asked Vince to turn over the shell casings. He waited while they were checked for fingerprints. There were prints on one set, none on the other.

"The sheriff's guys got all excited. You know, you can't load a rifle without leaving prints on the shell casings," he told me. "You got to pick up each one and put it in. So he must've worn gloves. No one's going to do that, except to conceal evidence. It's more proof. Somebody went up there expecting to kill Trooper."

I'd been right about how Trooper died. Was it really possible that the developers, or one of them, would go this far to protect an investment?

Reluctantly, I called Jimmy. He needed to know. I could hear him draw in a sharp breath when he learned that Trooper had been murdered. He was silent for almost a full minute. "I guess," he said finally, "that we've got one more thing to consider when we put together the news announcement about her death."

We did indeed.

It must have taken all of Jimmy's courage to carry out an

assignment he'd set for himself the next day: to meet with McCready, Wemmer, and Truesdale, and ask if he could lease land along Tengold Creek and behind City Hall. He'd known he was probably embarked on Mission Impossible, but Trooper had wanted him to give it a try. He was to offer a large sum of money; this was the site she most favored for the June hurrah.

McCready and Wemmer had listened to the proposal impassively. Truesdale, however, had shown considerable interest, which Jimmy at first had taken to be part of his habitual salesman demeanor.

"But that isn't how it was," Jimmy reported. "Truesdale was all ready to accept the deal—cash on the barrelhead. But before anyone else could say anything, McCready started laying on the *smooth*. I'd made a fine offer, he said, one that merited serious consideration. But of course I must realize that the partners would have to think it over. Et cetera. His usual blah, blah, blah. There's no way McCready will okay the deal."

I wondered what could have motivated Truesdale; he was clearly at odds with his partners on this point. Still, he'd wanted to sign on the dotted line—wanted to, in Jimmy's words, "hot and heavy." I could come up with dozens of theories but only one conclusion: I didn't have enough information about the man. Come next week, when we'd gotten past the hoo-ha scheduled for Sunday and I'd been to Trooper's place, I'd have to check a little more closely into the good Dr. T.

The week brought one more surprise.

When I'd gone to Spicer Realty to collect my check from Sam Jones, the secretary told me he'd phoned again. "He has another job for you," she said, wearing that closed look secretaries always have when they're covering up for their boss. "Mr. Spicer said I was to be sure to tell you this one also will pay top dollar."

Only the day before, Vince had announced he'd been hired for a special security job the coming weekend. "Jeez, I'm sorry I won't be in Buckeye to see Amos's Long Tom demonstration," he told me. "And the stagecoach. But I signed on to work security at the Camellia Festival. It's a special contract. We work on top of their regular security, and at a price too sweet to turn down—three days at top wages."

*Top wages*. Very much like *top dollar*. And, come to think of it, very much like Howie's plum assignment at the fertilizer plant.

I declined further assignments from Mr. Jones. Courteously.

▽

# 21

SATURDAY MORNING I drove out to Buckeye to have a private visit with Amos. I found him working in his barn, doing a last-minute spit-and-polish on the stagecoach.

"It looks beautiful," I told him.

The coach indeed looked resplendent, even inside the dim barn. Shafts of sunlight shone down on it through occasional holes in the old roof, and dust motes danced in the light. The brass and leather fittings gleamed and the wood was burnished to a high gloss; the air was redolent with leather conditioner. I felt a sudden surge of affection for Amos, for the stagecoach, and even for the barn, which reminded me of the barns of my childhood.

"It surely looks beautiful," I repeated.

"I got Prince and Pat—my horses—out in the pasture," Amos said. "They're chomping at the bit for another chance to pull her. A stagecoach is a tall order for a two-horse team, but they want to do it."

Another chance. "You've had the stagecoach out?"

"Sure. Took a trial spin yesterday, and another first thing this morning."

"Then your surprise for tomorrow won't be much of a surprise around Buckeye."

"Maybe. Maybe not. Folks around here don't pay much attention to what I do."

Except for his Sunday demonstrations, I thought. "Vince is worried about another case of sabotage," I said. "He can't be here this weekend."

"No need to worry this time. I got the Long Tom broke down into four sections, each hid in a different place. I won't put it together until the last minute."

"Frannie and I will be here early tomorrow. We could keep watch for you—stand guard over the Long Tom after it's assembled or keep an eye on the stagecoach."

"I'd be much obliged. We ought to be safe with the Long Tom. But the stagecoach . . ." He chuckled. "I can't break her up and put her in four different places."

"What precautions do you have in mind?"

"I'll check at the last minute to make sure there's no damage done—inspect the running gear, look at the harness and reins for cuts, that sort of thing. I'll make sure the wagon tongue's okay, too. We want the team and coach to stay together, the way they was meant to."

I studied the coach, noticing the long brake handle. It was equipped with hand-carved wooden brake shoes—brand new—that rested against the metal rims of the tall back wheels.

"Maybe somebody could do something to jigger the brakes," I suggested.

"I don't see how anybody could do it without me noticing."

Amos climbed up into the driver's seat. He put his foot in the brake stirrup; the brake shoe pushed against the rim. The mechanism was simple. "Maybe someone could sabotage the brakes by cutting into the brake lever," I said.

"Someone does that, I'd know it first time I used those brakes. A man gets to know the feel of his brakes. You got to have a just-right touch—light most of the time, but you put muscle into it on a downhill grade. You know, on some of these old routes, brake shoes could wear out mighty fast." Amos clambered down from the driver's seat. "Come on up to the house. I'll fix you a cup of coffee."

He escorted me through his back door and into his kitchen, the centerpiece of which was an old-fashioned wood-burning range. Beside the range, on a small table, was a two-burner electric stove. One wall of the kitchen was lined with open shelves, filled with cups and dishes, canned goods and cooking pots. The round dining table was covered with a red-and-white checked plastic tablecloth.

Amos took a kettle from the electric stove, replenished it with water, and put it back to heat.

"Hope you don't mind instant."

He set out two coffee mugs and two spoons, a jar of coffee, packets of creamer, and sugar. When the kettle began to whistle Amos supplied our coffee mugs with hot water. I settled into quizzing him about Palooka, which was the main reason I'd come this morning.

I was in luck. It turned out Amos had known Palooka ever since the Buckeye policeman was a boy.

"He and his mother moved here when he was in grammar school, maybe about fourth grade. Only he wasn't called Palooka then. It was Francis. Francis Patrick O'Rourke, and his mother always called him by his full name. She doted on the boy. I don't know where the father was; we never heard about him." He shook his head. "That boy needed a father. He was big for his age, even then."

"He must have had a tough time getting along with the other boys."

"He never did get along with them. They took to calling him Fran-sissy. The nickname stuck."

"Poor kid."

"Well, that boy was smart as a whip. He tried to hide it, but I could tell. He'd come see me sometimes, wanting to learn how to do things with tools, and to know how things were done in the old days, too. I liked him. But it was sad, a bright boy like him such an outcast."

Amos paused and took a long sip of coffee. I tried to imagine Palooka as a lonely overweight child.

"Things changed not long after he started high school. He took up boxing and slimmed down. We had a teacher back then who liked to coach boxing. And the boy was good, really worked at it."

It made perfect sense to me, the boxing. He'd no doubt been hazed by his classmates, probably taken his share of physical abuse. This was something he could do on his own, not a team sport where he'd have to be accepted by the other boys. And it would put them on notice to leave him alone. No more hazing.

"By the time young O'Rourke was a senior the rumor around town was that he was in line for an athletic scholarship. Everybody said one of those big colleges back East wanted him; they'd pay full expenses. But then his mom took sick. So Palooka—that's what everybody called him by then—stayed home. He quit boxing, began putting on weight."

"Is that when he became a Buckeye policeman?"

"Well, that happened pretty quick, but not right away, not until Mrs. O'Rourke died. The boy was working part time then, in the shop at the Wemmer agency. Not long after, McCready became city manager. He was the one who hired Palooka to be a policeman."

That was smart. McCready had an intelligent recruit, although an overweight one. More important, he'd done the young man a favor and could expect his loyalty.

I went back to the fact that Palooka had worked for Wemmer. "Was Mike Kelly working for Wemmer when Palooka worked there?" I asked.

"Yep. Matter of fact, that's why Palooka went to work for Wemmer. He and Kelly go way back. They moved into town the same year and were buddies all through school."

Kelly was probably the only boy who'd be willing to keep company with Fran-sissy, I thought, and then only because the two of them were outsiders.

"The two, Kelly and O'Rourke, made a strange pair," Amos went on. "It's even more strange now, being that they're still buddies." Amos shook his head, indicating his lack of understanding, and then tapped a finger to the side of his forehead. "Mike's not very bright, you know."

$\triangledown$

# 22

Sunday morning dawned bright and clear and beautiful—a perfect springtime day in the Mother Lode. The sky, rainwashed, was an astonishing blue and the grass in the fields an intense green.

Frannie, her earlier gloom forgotten, was eager to take a stagecoach ride. "Gracious!" she exclaimed, as we stood talking with Jimmy and Howie while Howie unloaded his photo equipment from the Volvo station wagon. "Riding in a real stagecoach! I'm so excited, I'm scarcely willing to wait through the Long Tom demonstration."

"Better not let Amos hear you say that," Howie said. He jerked a thumb toward Amos's truck, which was just pulling up.

Amos hopped out of the cab. He wore new blue jeans and a bright red bandana tucked into the collar of his denim shirt. Also—apparently in honor of the spring day—he had on a straw hat. He climbed into the back of his truck and began unloading the components of the Long Tom. Jimmy and Howie hurried over to help him.

I followed. "Do you want Frannie and me to go over and keep an eye on your stagecoach?" I asked Amos.

He pushed the straw hat back on his head. "Sure thing," he said. "I was hoping you two would get here in time to stand watch over it."

Frannie and I drove over to Amos's place, which she'd never seen, and parked by the old barn.

"Isn't this a wonderful adventure!" Frannie hugged her

elbows with excitement as she waited for me to open one side of the barn's double doors. "Oh!" she exclaimed, stepping inside. "Just look at all those beautiful old things. And the stagecoach! It's marvelous!"

It was—if possible—more burnished and polished than yesterday. The smell of leather conditioner was in the air, also the fragrance of newly cut lumber.

Frannie moved over to the coach and ran her fingers tentatively along one spoke of a wheel. Then she moved to the passenger compartment door and, on tiptoe, tried to peer inside. She glanced around. Nearby was a homemade wooden stool, no doubt intended by Amos as a mounting block for the coach. Frannie dragged it over, climbed up, and reached for the door handle.

"Watch out!" I commanded in my sternest tones. "There might be a rattlesnake in there."

She shrieked. Her hand recoiled from the door handle and she almost lost her balance.

I quickly stepped forward to steady her. "I'm sorry, I couldn't help myself. The temptation was too much."

"Emma! You . . . !" Frannie's eyes flashed. From her advantage on the stool she waggled a finger in my face. "You . . . *you!*" She was sputtering, too angry to say more.

"I'm sorry, Frannie," I repeated as I helped her down.

I shouldn't have made a joke about this, I realized. But after the week we'd all experienced, something to laugh about had a lot of appeal. I put an arm across Frannie's shoulders and gave her a quick hug. "That was wrong. I *am* sorry."

Amos arrived.

"Just an hour to go until the demonstration," he announced, sounding triumphant. He proffered a white paper bag. "Hamburgers, from Marie's Doughnut Shop."

"Gracious! How nice of you."

"Thank you very much," I echoed.

"Don't thank me, thank Howie." Amos arrayed three wrapped hamburgers on the little stool, and beside them three containers of coffee. "Howie says he's feeling rich these days, what with that assignment he had."

"Well, it's very nice of him," Frannie said.

"It sure is," I chimed in. "By the way, I was glad to see Howie here today. He's going to take more publicity photos?"

"He sure is."

I wondered whether Howie had been offered another out-of-town assignment. If he had, he must have put them off. We were a team now, eager to do anything to make the hurrah a success. "I'm glad he's going to be around. We need some good stagecoach photos."

"We'll get 'em. Howie says he's going to catch everything with the Long Tom first, then do pictures of the stagecoach in action."

"Oh, how nice!"

"Real nice," Amos said. "He's looking to get some shots of Pat and Prince pulling the coach, and he'll make enlargements for me to keep."

"Pat and Prince?" Frannie asked.

"My horses. They'll be pulling the coach."

"Oooh! Can I go on the first ride?"

"Sure thing."

Amos kept his promise.

When he'd finished the Long Tom demonstration—to cheers from a sizable crowd—he announced the stagecoach rides. The crowd, as instructed, waited in line where Amos had placed the homemade footstool while he went to fetch the stagecoach. Before the demonstration he'd brought it from his barn up to City Hall and positioned it around the corner, just out of sight of the crowd assembled in the parking lot. I'd spent the time during the demonstration keeping an eye on the coach, and making friends with Prince and Pat.

As soon as Amos had the coach ready he called to Frannie from his perch on the driver's seat.

"This lady is a special passenger," he announced to those waiting in line. "Let her on first."

Those at the front of the line exchanged impatient

glances. Frannie put a foot on the stool, then looked up at the closed door of the passenger compartment.

I moved forward and opened the door. "Step right up," I said in what I hoped was a passable imitation of Trooper's speaking-to-the-crowd voice. I reached over, caught Frannie by the elbow, and gave her a boost up into the passenger compartment.

The coach rocked gently forward and back as Frannie got in. She let out an "Oooh!" at the unexpected motion, and then lurched to the far side and more or less dropped onto the forward-facing seat.

Howie, who had hurried around to the opposite side of the stagecoach, called out to Frannie to look out the window and wave at him. I continued in my role as door attendant, assisting five more passengers up and into the coach.

"That's it for this trip," Amos announced. "But you're not going to go away disappointed. I can't take more than six at a time—I only have two horses. But you'll get your rides, don't worry. We've got all afternoon."

Amos nodded at me and indicated I should move the footstool. I picked it up, trying my best for a showman's style, and set it safely back from the stagecoach. "The line starts here for the next ride," I announced. "Keep your order and move over."

Amos gave a tip of his hat to me. "Thank you, Emma. Thank you, folks." He put the hat back on. "Now, this here's an 1868 Concord stagecoach, once used on the old Buckeye-to-Leona route. With a full complement of horses, it'd go six miles an hour on the level grade, a lot slower on the hills— slower still if there was passengers up on top."

"Or maybe a heavy shipment of gold," someone from the audience volunteered.

"Yessir," Amos said smoothly, "these coaches carried gold shipments along with passengers and their luggage. You could put nine inside and seven more on top, hanging on for dear life."

He was beginning to look and sound like a pro, I thought,

with his hat pushed back on his head, his foot resting lightly in the brake stirrup.

"Amos!" Howie called out. "I want to get some more shots before you leave." He photographed Amos holding the reins, then backed up for a shot of the horses and stagecoach. "Everybody wave!" he hollered.

The passengers waved eagerly out the windows.

"Everyone all set back there?" Amos called as soon as Howie had finished taking pictures. He waited a moment, then clucked at the horses and gave a slap with the reins. The crowd cheered and the coach started smoothly, with a slight forward-and-back rolling motion and a great deal of creaking. The harness jangled, the horses' hooves sounded smartly on the parking lot pavement.

As the coach reached the far end of the parking lot, Amos began easing it onto City Hall Drive, all the while calling words of encouragement to Pat and Prince. I heard a faint scrape of brakes against the wheel rims as he slowed just before the turn. Then the coach, rolling with a majestic rhythm, started down the gentle hill. At Buckeye Boulevard Amos eased into the turn, not wanting the stagecoach to move too fast on the steeper slope. But suddenly the coach lurched forward.

Amos gave a startled yell. "Whoa!"

He tried to work the brake lever, but the coach was out of control, lurching wildly as it careened down the steep hill toward Highway 18.

"Whoa!" Amos yelled again. And then, "Gee! Gee! Gee!" He pulled hard on the right-side reins.

It took me a moment to understand what he was trying to do: turn onto the level ground of the doughnut shop parking lot in an attempt to bring the coach to a stop.

"Gee!" Amos yelled again.

The horses, wild-eyed, veered to the right at the last possible moment and lurched around the turn. The coach careened crazily; I could hear shrieks and screams. I started running across the City Hall lot and down City Hall Drive.

The crowd followed, yelling and scrambling behind me.

I was certain the coach would tip over as it made the turn into the doughnut shop lot, but after wobbling on two wheels for what seemed like an eternity, it righted. Lurching and swaying, it lumbered across the space in front of the restaurant and started into the turn behind the kitchen.

The stagecoach will make it, I said to myself over and over again. Amos still had control of the horses, so things were going to be okay. Frannie would be safe. By now I could see what Amos had in mind. He was going to run the coach along the sloping hillside to slow it, then come back to level ground. The stagecoach will make it, I told myself. Everything will be all right. He'll bring the coach to a stop.

I was wrong.

The coach swayed, tottered, almost righted itself, but then lost balance and tipped, scraping against the hillside. It came to a stop half tipped over and resting against a rock outcropping. Two wheels were in the air, turning slowly.

Dear Lord! Don't let Frannie be hurt.

I broke into a run. By the time I reached the stagecoach, Amos had managed to get down to the ground and was trying to get his horses unhitched. Both animals were terribly agitated, their flanks trembling and their eyes rolling, but Pat was by far the more out of control. His front feet pranced; he seemed about to leap forward. Amos was somehow managing to keep a hold on him, stroking the side of Pat's face and speaking in soothing tones. The people inside the coach shouted for help; apparently the door was jammed. Their movements rocked the coach, threatening at any moment to destroy its precarious balance.

Howie's station wagon screeched into the doughnut shop lot. I motioned him to bring his vehicle over so we could use it as a rescue platform, then turned my attention back to the passengers. "Hold on," I called. "We'll get you out in a minute."

As soon as Howie had the station wagon in position I climbed up on the roof and began pulling on the stagecoach door handle. With help from someone pushing from the inside, I managed to get the door open. By this time, a burly man from the City Hall crowd was up there beside me. We began pulling out passengers. Frannie, safe and sound, was the first.

As we continued to pull passengers up through the narrow stagecoach door, my attention was caught by a stubby figure standing just outside the restaurant kitchen. It was Aggie, her apron-wrapped form immobile with disapproval, her hands on her hips. She was the embodiment of scorn—the personification, I thought, of Buckeye's hostility toward the hurrah and anyone associated with it.

▽

## 23

As soon as the passengers—none of them seriously harmed—were out of the stagecoach, Aggie disappeared back into her kitchen. Moments later the Buckeye patrol car, lights flashing, started down the hill. No coincidence, I thought.

By this time Amos had gotten the horses soothed, unhitched, and safely tethered to the fence. He headed for the stagecoach.

"What happened to the brakes?" I asked, following beside him.

"I don't know, but I surely intend to find out."

Howie pulled his station wagon away from the stagecoach and returned with his camera; Amos began examining the brakes.

"Let's get the coach righted in a hurry," I said, "before the local officials have a chance to say we're not supposed to— that we have to leave evidence where it is." I gestured toward the arriving police car.

Amos moved swiftly. "Jimmy, give me a hand," he called.

To my surprise, the two of them had the coach righted by the time Palooka O'Rourke, notebook in hand, had managed to climb out of his car and lumber over. He greeted us curtly—the same harsh voice he'd used when he'd asked me what kind of oil was in the Long Tom—and gestured with his notebook toward Howie. "Tell your friend the Buckeye Police Department will want those photos."

"Okay," I said, chilled by his unsympathetic manner.

Amos, still inspecting the stagecoach, scowled, then reached out and pulled the remains of the brakes from the nearest rear wheel. He broke off a fragment of the wooden shoe and showed it to us. "Look!" he said, his face red with anger. It was merely a shell. The outside was smooth, the inside hollowed out. It showed the marks of a router.

By now everyone had crowded close, trying to see over our shoulders and around Palooka's girth.

"What's that?" Palooka growled.

"It's what's left of my brakes—brand-new brake shoes. I'd just made them. Someone came sneaking into my barn and routed them out."

I heard Palooka draw in a sharp breath.

"Damned fool," Amos went on, "whoever did it. Could've gotten people killed!"

"I know when the brake shoes could have been sabotaged," I suggested to Amos. "When you brought the Long Tom over to City Hall there must have been at least ten minutes before Frannie and I went to keep watch in the barn." Someone, I thought, would have had to have been watching Amos every minute, just waiting for the chance.

Palooka looked at me long and steadily; I got the impression my judgment was being questioned. He started to write in his notebook, then stopped. "So in ten minutes," he said, "somebody sneaked into Amos's barn, found a place to plug in a router, got the brake shoes off—"

I noticed the harshness was gone from Palooka's voice. In fact, he sounded relaxed, almost as if his mind had been relieved of some unhappy burden.

"—and then routed out the shoes and reinstalled them," Palooka went on. "And no one heard the noise of the router. By the way, Mrs. Chizzit, did you notice any fresh wood shavings on the barn floor?"

He had a point. "No," I said.

An instant later I remembered smelling freshly cut wood when I was in the barn this morning. I was about to say so when Amos spoke up.

"Say," he said, sounding puzzled. "There's something . . . ," He was still holding the fragment of the brake shoe, turning it one way and another. "The grain of the wood is different, and"—he took time out to sniff it—"I used oak and this is alder. This isn't the brake shoe I made."

"Someone must have switched brake shoes," I declared. "That would be quieter and quicker." I cast a look at Palooka. "Neater, too. No wood shavings."

Palooka stared back at me. The muscles around his eyes tightened. After a moment he turned to Amos. "You sure this isn't the brake shoe you made?" he asked. The harshness was back in his voice. "Dead sure?" He tapped his notebook with his pencil. "Court-of-law sure?"

Amos stood his ground. "Yes," he said firmly. "Court-of-law sure."

Palooka's attitude was condescending, like McCready's. Especially with the "Mrs. Chizzit" business. He was putting me down, and Amos, the man who'd been so kind to him when he was a boy. He was on the defensive, but why?

The light dawned. Kelly.

He thought Kelly was responsible for the gouged-out brake shoes. Ditto with the Long Tom and the rattlesnake incident. It made sense—Palooka had probably been looking out for Kelly ever since fourth grade. But would he suppress evidence to protect his friend?

"Howie," I called, motioning him over. "Come take a photo of this." ·

Palooka watched in impassive silence as Howie took pictures of the brake shoe.

Palooka continued his questioning. "Amos, I want you to tell me, start to finish, what happened here today."

Amos squinted up at Palooka, as if trying to see past that inscrutable expression. He repeated the story of the stage-coach ride. Palooka—once the lonely Fran-sissy—made notes. And I thought of the hours Amos must have invested in Palooka all those years ago.

"And would you say none of the passengers were seriously

injured?" Palooka asked at the conclusion of Amos's recital of events.

Amos cast a worried glance over to where the passengers huddled, waiting for the police business to be concluded. "Don't think so."

"And your horses?"

"Scared, but they'll be okay. I should be over there with them right now."

"Now, how about damage to the stagecoach?" By this time, Palooka's voice had taken on a softer, more sympathetic tone.

"Don't rightly know yet. She's just scraped some, I think. I haven't had a chance to take a good look."

At that moment a distant siren began to sound. It seemed to me the noise came from the the direction of Buckeye's downtown. Palooka, without another word, closed his notebook, got into his patrol car, and headed back toward City Hall.

"What's happening?" I asked Amos.

"That's the fire department alarm. They got a stationary siren to call the volunteers."

"I wonder where . . . ," I said, looking around.

We spotted the plume of smoke at the same time. It was coming from somewhere along the far side of Highway 18. Amos grabbed me by the arm. "It looks like my place. We got to get going!"

"But what about Prince and Pat?"

Amos glanced from the plume of smoke, rapidly growing larger, to his team, stomping restlessly where they were tethered. Anguish contorted his face. "I got to take care of my animals."

# 24

Howie, Jimmy, Frannie, and I piled into Howie's station wagon. As we pulled out of the doughnut shop lot I gave a quick backward glance at Amos. He'd already started tending Pat and Prince. Somehow I thought he seemed older, more stooped . . . almost defeated. Then I told myself I had too active an imagination. But I was glad I'd given him a quick hug—condolence and farewell mixed together.

By the time we got onto Highway 18, I had no doubt the fire was at Amos's place. The plume of smoke had enlarged enormously and become a towering black chimney. As we approached the driveway we could see that his barn was afire. The entire back wall was ablaze.

The volunteer fire department siren still wailed, but there was no truck yet in evidence. Cars on Highway 18 were slowing; the drivers were gawking at the fire.

Howie pulled off the highway at Amos's driveway and parked well to one side in order to leave room for the fire fighters when they arrived. We got out of the station wagon and started toward the barn, then stopped when a gust of wind billowed smoke toward us. The heat was intense. Jimmy and Howie hesitated, took a few tentative steps forward, then stopped.

"There's no way we'll be able to salvage anything out of that barn," I said.

"Oh! This is terrible!" Frannie wailed. "Amos is going to lose all his beautiful treasures!"

She made as if to start toward the barn. I held her back.

We heard the wail of a fire truck siren.

"Do you suppose Amos has a garden hose somewhere?" Frannie asked. This time she started toward the weed-grown remains of a flower garden alongside Amos's house.

"Let's try back here." I headed for the rear porch. "Amos has a vegetable garden."

Jimmy, galvanized at last into action, dashed ahead of me. "I see the garden hose!" He grabbed the neat coil that lay on the ground near the porch and looked around as if uncertain what to do next.

By this time a truck from the volunteer fire department, its siren winding down, was turning in from the highway. Jimmy abandoned the garden hose; he and Howie ran to meet the firemen. I took over where Jimmy had left off and began unwinding the hose.

Frannie was right behind me. "Look. It's still connected to the faucet." She took the hose from me, tugging it in the direction of the fire. "Turn on the water," she called.

I hurried to the faucet; Frannie pulled at the hose.

"It's too far, I can't reach the barn," she shouted. "Maybe I can save the fence."

"Good! You better wet down the back porch, too. And all along the back of the house."

She nodded her understanding, then got out her handkerchief and wet it with water from the hose. Dodging billows of smoke and holding the handkerchief over her face with one hand, she began wetting down the fence and yard.

The fire truck had bumped to a hurried stop in mid-driveway. Two firemen leaped out. "Amos has a well here," one yelled to the other. "I'll grab the draft hose and siphon from it. You take the forward nozzle."

Jimmy and Howie stood by the driveway, poised to help, moving restlessly. "Anybody in that barn?" the fireman who'd given the orders shouted at them. "Amos isn't home, is he?"

Jimmy shook his head. "No!"

Palooka arrived, pulling his patrol car into the front yard. He beckoned urgently to Jimmy and Howie. "Get up on the road! Wave the cars by—highway patrol's on the way." Howie and Jimmy ran up the driveway. Palooka extracted his Polaroid camera from the patrol car and headed toward the barn.

A pickup truck screeched to a stop behind the patrol car. Another volunteer sprang out and hurried to help the fire fighter at the well, who was struggling to move the heavy wooden cover. I scurried across the driveway, steering clear of the fire truck and the hoses. More volunteers arrived as I quickly made my way toward the side of the barn away from the house. If there was any evidence of arson to find, I wanted to be the one to find it.

On the other side of the driveway I encountered tall grass and a thick hedge of Japanese quince. Slow going, but I plowed through, staying as far way from the barn as I could, near to Amos's property line. The blaze was moving fast. Flames licked out between the boards of the barn's side wall; they'd now reached nearly halfway to the front of the structure.

I closed my eyes momentarily, pained by the thought of that beautiful old barn and everything in it going up in smoke. This was Amos's workroom, his storehouse for everything he loved and had preserved so carefully. It was his treasury, his legacy, his life.

I couldn't ignore the heat from the roaring blaze, the choking smoke, the pops and crackles of destruction, but I pushed on, keeping my distance from the barn as best I could. At the far corner of the barn I spotted Amos's metal wheelbarrow. It was way over by the property line fence, far enough away so that it wasn't likely to be affected by the fire. And in the wheelbarrow I found a piece of folded paper, weighted down with a brick: another "Don't tread on me" note.

I left the note where it was and moved toward the back of the barn. Here I discovered a red gasoline can tossed into the high green grass. As I started toward it, Palooka showed up, Polaroid camera in hand.

I pointed to the gasoline can and shouted above the noise of the fire. "Evidence!"

He hurried over and photographed it at close range, then

backed off to get a shot that would show the discarded can in relation to the barn. At least he was doing his job, I thought. I left him to it, skirting the back corner of the barn where two fire fighters had positioned themselves to pour water through gaping holes in the back wall. I kept moving until I stood at some distance from the barn. The heat was intense, even though the wind was at my back, blowing the flames and smoke away from me.

The barn and everything in it would soon be consumed. Poor Amos! I wondered if he was still tending his horses, helplessly watching the smoke rise into the sky. This would be a terrible blow to him. And to the hurrah, too. With Trooper gone, we had begun more and more to depend on him, his dedication and enthusiasm, his steadfastness.

What would happen now?

I studied the burning beams—great thick slabs, possibly a century old. Tongues of flames licked out from the blackened wood; in many places the beams glowed from within, fiercely red. And the roof shingles were almost all consumed, the last few flaming shreds blowing away in the wind.

The upper part of the back wall moved inward, wavering unsteadily. The roof timbers buckled. The wall miraculously steadied, seeming to be supported by nothing more than flames.

The fire fighters shouted back and forth. I listened, still watching the fire, almost in a trance.

"Watch it!" one of the firemen shouted at me. "She's gonna go!"

The wall of the barn moved slowly inward, then fell with a whooshing rush. Flame and smoke plumed; a torrent of sparks showered. Another whoosh, and the near portion of the side wall folded inward, sending up even more sparks.

Still I looked, utterly fascinated.

"Lady! Chrissakes!" A fireman pulled me. I stumbled back to a safer distance.

The fire fighters at the back of the barn now aimed their hoses low, at the hot core of the fire.

"Joe's gonna stay on the hot spots," one shouted. "Put hose number three on the house. Hey! Get the other old lady out of the way."

Frannie.

I felt a sudden need to be the one who escorted her to a safe spot; she didn't need some stranger shouting at her. I hurried up the path from barn to kitchen. The air was thick with steam and smoke; behind me the flames still produced a muted hiss and crackle.

Frannie sat on the back porch steps, the garden hose in her hand. "Come on," I said, prying it from her grasp. "Let's go around to the front of the house. The firemen will take care of things here now."

I walked her with me, around the side of the house, heading toward the front porch steps. At this moment Amos arrived in his pickup, pulling to a tire-grinding stop in the driveway. He stepped out hurriedly. For a moment, I thought he was going to run straight toward the burning remains of the barn. He took a step, then stopped, stunned. His knees almost buckled; he reached back to the open door of his truck to steady himself, laying his arm across the top. He turned to stare incredulously at the flaming ruin for a long moment, then leaned against the truck door and hid his face against his arm.

One of the firemen came and led him away. As they walked down the driveway I could see Amos's shoulders begin to heave.

I looked at Frannie. Tears streamed down her cheeks. I realized my face was wet, too.

"My eyes hurt from the smoke," I said foolishly. Then I sat down beside her, buried my face in my hands, and cried outright.

$\triangledown$

# 25

I DON'T KNOW how long it was that Frannie and I sat side by side on Amos's porch. It was a relief to be no longer watching the flames, but we could hear great whooshes as the last chunks of the barn's pillars fell. I could well imagine what remained: a smoking expanse of coals filmed over with a layer of gray ash, blackened stubs of upright beams, and the occasional metal skeleton of this or that treasure.

I took hold of Frannie's hand. "You did a good job, keeping the fence and the yard wet."

She nodded. "The firemen are taking care of the sparks now. With their big hoses." She sighed. "I turned off the garden hose a little while ago."

"Still, you did a good job."

"Mmmm." Frannie was silent. Presently she stirred, then sadly shook her head. "This is going to be just terrible for Amos."

I agreed, remembering from this morning the jaunty red bandana, the new blue jeans and the straw hat, and then the last image of Amos, the firemen leading him away. I was silent, trying to gather my thoughts and my energy. We ought to help him. I numbly began working on the logistics of moving the stagecoach. We'd have to jury-rig something for the brakes. Under any other circumstances, Amos would make new brakes in his shop. But his shop and all his tools had been destroyed by the fire. And I wondered about his horses, where he'd keep them. The weather was mild, the cold of winter gone—I guessed they could be brought home and tethered outdoors.

"You don't suppose," Frannie ventured, "that Amos would accept an invitation to stay at my house for a few days."

"I doubt it. I don't know. I suppose he'll want to start straightening out things here."

"Oh, look! Here come Howie and Jimmy."

They were trudging in at the driveway.

"Yoohoo! We're over here," Frannie called.

Howie and Jimmy picked up their pace, hurrying toward the front porch.

A moment later McCready arrived in his big Chrysler. He parked beside Palooka's patrol car, greeted the firemen, and went toward the barn site, presumably in search of Palooka.

Howie and Jimmy dropped onto the porch steps beside us. "Whew!" Howie said. "I think people zone out when they see a fire."

"Yeah," Jimmy agreed. "You motion them on and they just sit there. And the highway patrol didn't show up until just now."

They both looked bushed. "You want a drink of water?" I asked.

Jimmy glanced toward the house. "Yeah, sure. But we can find our way around inside. We'll get it for ourselves." He and Howie disappeared inside.

A moment later McCready started up the path toward us. I nudged Frannie.

For some reason, we both stood as McCready reached the porch. "Something I can do for you?" I asked. I was feeling hostile and too tired to make any bones about it.

I got the impression he'd been about to shake hands, but then had thought better of it. "Good afternoon, Mrs. Chizzit." He nodded to Frannie. "Mrs. Edmundson."

"Actually," I said, "it's not a very good afternoon."

"No, it isn't, is it?" He shook his head, putting on a sad expression. "A terrible tragedy, terrible. This has been a most unfortunate afternoon for poor Amos . . . first the mishap with the stagecoach, and now this." He swept his hand in the direction of the barn, and put on an even more mournful expression than before.

"Just exactly what did you need with us?" I asked.

"Well . . ." He straightened, seeming to gather his thoughts. "Um . . . I don't *need* anything of you, Mrs. Chizzit. But I wanted to thank you—and Mrs. Edmundson, too—for your prompt action this afternoon. You've been most helpful."

I looked at him coldly, saying nothing.

"I wanted you to know," he went on slowly, "that Amos has the support of the community behind him in this terrible time of tragedy."

"What kind of support?" I asked.

"To begin with, Father Cydzik, our local priest, has offered the use of the old stable behind the parish hall for Amos's horses. Amos is one of his parishioners, you know."

"That was nice of Father Cydzik." I was relieved to know that at least one person cared enough to help.

"All the citizens here in Buckeye believe in coming forward when a neighbor is in need," McCready went on. He allowed himself a tight little smile. "As for the city of Buckeye itself, we believe in lending a helping hand."

I felt like saying No kidding.

"We have used city equipment," McCready went on smoothly, "to bring the damaged stagecoach back to the City Hall area. Amos is free to store it in our corporation yard for as long as necessary, for however long it takes for him to replace the building he's lost here."

It was my turn to do a tight little smile.

"The barn is irreplaceable."

"Well, yes, of course. All those artifacts in it and so forth."

By this time Jimmy and Howie had come back onto the porch. McCready turned his attention to them.

He offered a limp handshake to Jimmy. "I understand you have a new position with a project the late Mrs. Hadley started. Congratulations."

"Thanks," Jimmy mumbled.

"And I don't believe I've met your friend." McCready offered his handshake to Howie. "Jonathan McCready, Buckeye's city manager."

Maybe McCready hadn't met Howie, I thought, but he sure as heck knew who he was. McCready had to have arranged his stay-away-from-Buckeye assignments, as well as the phony jobs for me and Vince. He was the one with the connections and resources to do it.

"Well!" McCready went on with patently false enthusiasm, "you two were certainly helpful. I'm told you did an excellent job directing traffic."

Frannie nudged me. "Sugar wouldn't melt . . . ," she muttered with quiet vehemence.

If he heard her, McCready didn't let on. "It's time for me to be running along now. I want to pay my respects to Amos before I leave. *Such* a tragedy this afternoon—a double tragedy, nearly, what with the stagecoach thing." He paused, then looked me straight in the eye. "There was a real potential for disaster there, which I'm glad didn't materialize." He started down the steps, then turned back. "By the way, Jimmy, you really ought to look into liability insurance if Amos undertakes any further excursions with that stagecoach of his." He shook his head with the air of a parent quietly tolerating the foolish behavior of a child. "There are so many complications to matters like this." He turned on his heel and left.

So *that* was his agenda: intimidate us, make us think we weren't up to handling anything complex. But McCready knew an Achilles' heel when he saw one—we'd be in deep trouble if one of the stagecoach passengers decided to sue.

"Wow!" Howie said. "Some parting shot."

Jimmy looked pale. "We should have thought about insurance for today. Of course, it's in the plans for the hurrah, but—"

"Gracious! You don't suppose he'd actually put somebody up to filing a lawsuit against poor Amos, do you?"

"Probably not," Jimmy said thoughtfully, "but only because

he'd be taking too much risk of getting found out at it."

"But he'd like to convince us that the hurrah is more of a challenge than we can handle," I said.

The four of us sat in silence, staring glumly at the smoke and steam that from time to time drifted from the barn up the driveway.

Before long the firemen who'd arrived in pickup trucks were making noisy goodbyes, then backing out the driveway with a great deal of engine-revving and gravel-spewing. Only the big truck and the two original fire fighters remained.

"It's all over." Frannie shook her head sadly.

"You mean the fire, don't you?" I asked. "Not the hurrah."

"Certainly not the hurrah!" Frannie looked shocked that I would say such a thing. "We *have* to make that work."

"Yes, we do," Jimmy said. "We will, too."

"You and Trooper did a lot of planning," I said to Jimmy. "I think we ought to all get together, as soon as we can, and go over the plans. This is going to be tough to pull off. Not only do we have to do it without Trooper, but we also have to do it without everything that was in that barn."

"We still have the stagecoach," Frannie pointed out. "Don't you worry. We'll get it all taken care of."

"By June," I reminded her.

"By June," she affirmed.

"Speaking of work to be done," Jimmy said, "there's a bunch of stuff down in Trooper's apartment in Los Angeles that we're going to need. Her computer files, bank statements, that kind of thing. And she said her life insurance policy is down there, too." He was looking straight at me.

"You want me to go." I made it a statement, not a question.

"Right."

"Sure, anytime."

"Well, I was going to tell you earlier, before everything started to go wrong. We need this stuff . . . like yesterday."

"So?"

Without another word, Jimmy pulled a folded-up envelope

from his shirt pocket and handed it to me. "Airline tickets. They're for tomorrow."

This was a surprise. I'd been counting on tomorrow to do other things. First and foremost, I wanted to help Amos if I could. I also needed to check with Vince to see what he'd learned about Truesdale. And I wanted to do some research on my own about the proposed annexation.

"You'll have time to get ready in the morning. The flight doesn't leave until ten o'clock," Jimmy said. "I really can't be the one to go. I've got to stay on top of things here."

"But . . ."

"Oh, for heaven's sake, Emma. Go!"

I agreed to do it.

Jimmy brought forth a set of apartment keys. "The address is in the ticket envelope," he said, "along with a list of stuff I need. Most of all, don't forget that life insurance policy. It's important."

"Okay." I looked at everything briefly, refolded the envelope and put it in my shirt pocket, all the while wondering why Trooper's life insurance policy should be so important.

Another truck pulled into the driveway. It had a California Department of Forestry insignia on the door; a man in uniform got out and started walking toward the barn.

"Why do you suppose this guy is here?" Howie asked.

"I know him," Jimmy said. "He's Arthur Ernest, the CDF investigator. Nice guy. He helped me with a fire-prevention story last fall."

"Good enough," I said. "This fire definitely needs investigation. By an expert." And, I added to myself, somebody who's not connected to the Buckeye glitterati.

"What makes you say that?" Jimmy asked. "Do you think they'll find evidence of arson?"

"They darn well should. Over there beyond the barn I found two things: a 'Don't tread on me' note and an empty gasoline can."

Howie gave a long, low whistle. "I better get photos of this stuff."

"Palooka took Polaroid pictures of the gas can," I said as the four of us moved off the porch and toward the driveway. "I didn't stick around to see, but I guess he found the note, too."

"Look!" Frannie exclaimed. "Palooka's showing the gasoline can to the inspector now."

Palooka was indeed displaying the can, all neatly bundled in a plastic evidence bag.

"Does he have the 'Don't tread on me' note, too?" Jimmy asked.

"I don't know, but he had to have found it in Amos's wheelbarrow. That wheelbarrow pretty much said, Come look at me. It was over by the property fence, a good distance from the fire. Plus it was in the high grass and obviously recently put there."

"Let's go see if the wheelbarrow's still there," Howie said. "On the way, I'll get my camera out of the station wagon."

We trooped over to the wagon, Howie in the lead. As we approached it, he let out a yell.

"What's the matter?" I called.

"Look for yourself!"

The back of the wagon was up. Inside, every camera case was open. And festooned in milky beige streamers around the interior were rolls and rolls of exposed film.

# 26

SUNDAY NIGHT I sat by the telephone collecting my thoughts. I'd left Buckeye without having a chance to talk to Amos; I wanted to let him know how sorry I was about everything he'd lost.

The phone rang.

"I'm all done at the camellia show," Vince announced. "Jeez! You ought see the size of the paycheck I walked away with."

I racked my brain for some easy way to tell him what had happened today in Buckeye, but I felt used up, too tired to think. "That's nice, Vince," I said dully.

"Hey!" His voice registered sudden alarm. "Something went wrong. What happened? Jeez! I shoulda been there! I *knew* I shoulda been there!"

"Well, to begin with, somebody sabotaged the brakes on Amos's stagecoach."

"I shoulda been there," Vince repeated dolefully.

"You couldn't have prevented it, Vince. All it took was ten minutes, no one watching for just—"

"Aw! I never should've taken this other job."

"Just ten minutes," I repeated. "It could have happened even if you *had* been there. Besides, Amos got the stagecoach stopped with no one hurt."

"Aw . . . no! The stagecoach crashed?"

I told him about it, starting with what had happened to the stagecoach brakes and working my way through to the loss of Amos's barn and everything in it.

"Poor Amos," Vince said softly when I had finished.

Neither of us spoke for a few moments.

"At least the local priest gave Amos a place to keep his horses," I said. I wondered if there had been any other offers of help. I discounted McCready's letting Amos store his stagecoach on city premises as an act of charity-for-display. Which hadn't cost McCready a dime.

"Jeez! Isn't anybody else helping Amos?"

"I don't know. There was nothing I knew of by the time I brought Frannie home." If it weren't for the town's hostility, I thought, Amos's kitchen counter would have been heaped with covered dishes and casseroles, and the lawn stacked three-deep with neighbors offering their help.

"I should be out there right now," Vince said. "There'll be something I could do."

"It's a two-hour drive from Fairville to Buckeye," I said. "No sense you going until tomorrow."

"Yeah. I suppose." Vince lapsed into silence.

Vince's presence would be welcome tomorrow, I thought. For moral support, if for no other reason. "Amos will be glad to see you," I said. "Jimmy, too."

"Yeah. Oh, I almost forgot to tell you."

"Tell me what?"

"You wanted me to dig up financial dirt, see what else I could pick up on any of the Buckeye people."

"Yes, I did." I reached for my notepad and pencil. "What did you learn?"

"Well, nuthin' more on Trooper. Remember? You asked, after her personal files came up empty, to check the business stuff. You thought she might be living out of the business. Moneywise, I mean."

"Right."

"Well, like I said, still nuthin'. The business doesn't own any property, and the only address is the one for her apartment."

"Thanks for trying. I should be able to find out more tomorrow, anyway, when I go down to Los Angeles."

"Los Angeles? You're not coming to Buckeye tomorrow?"

"No. Jimmy asked me to bring back things from Trooper's apartment."

"You want me to come with you?"

"No, thanks, Vince. I think you'd be a lot more useful in Buckeye."

"Aw." He sighed heavily. "You're probably right." Another sigh. "Say, I did turn up something new in the financial department."

"About Trooper?"

"Naw. About that Truesdale guy. About a year ago, Truesdale took out a mortgage on his house—not for full value, but a big chunk."

"How big a chunk?"

"Fifty thousand. Before that he owned the house free and clear, had for years—rumor has it that his first wife's money paid for building it."

She must have been singularly lacking in taste, I thought, to have subsidized that monstrosity. Or completely under Truesdale's thumb. "What do you suppose he wanted the money for?" I asked.

"I dunno. But he wasn't advertising that he borrowed it. Took out the loan with an outfit in Stockton. Wait a minute."

Vince shuffled papers.

"Here it is. Inland Empire Mortgage Company. Fifty thousand, to Cecil P. Truesdale." Vince giggled. "No wonder he calls himself Doc."

"Isn't his wife's name on the loan—the wife he has now?"

"Nope, just him. The house was his separate property."

"Right." I wondered if he and the present Mrs. T. were already married when he took out the loan. Maybe not, I thought. Maybe the money was for the gallant and charming Cecil Truesdale to go wife hunting.

How much would it take? A new wardrobe would set him back some, even if his tastes did run to polyester. Tickets for an expensive cruise, maybe. His new car. Still, fifty thousand seemed like a lot. Of course, he'd have to keep up the impression. Occasional excursions. Fancy meals. Evenings out. And he couldn't count on finding a suitable wealthy widow the first time around. He'd have to have money in reserve.

"Vince, when you're in Buckeye tomorrow, maybe you can find out how long the Truesdales have been married. I bet you could have coffee again with Mrs. T."

"Well, I suppose." He sounded reluctant.

"Sounds to me like you don't want to trade on your friendship with her, ask her a lot of questions and so forth."

"Yeah," Vince mumbled. "You got it."

"Well, didn't she ask you a bunch of questions?"

Silence.

"Think like a policeman, Vince," I said.

More silence. "Yeah. I get your point."

"Thanks, Vince. And I'll see you after I'm back from Los Angeles. Oh, I almost forgot. You're invited to Frannie's house tomorrow night. She wants everybody to come for supper."

After I'd hung up I again spent a few moments collecting myself to talk with Amos, then dialed his number. I was very surprised, when he answered the phone, to hear in the background the rousing strains of a John Philip Sousa march.

"Wait a minute," Amos told me, sounding not the least bit disconsolate. "I'll turn down the phonograph."

I waited, puzzled. The music abated after a moment and I heard Amos tell someone it was me on the phone.

"Sorry," Amos said when he came back on the line. "Jimmy was practicing a routine with his cane and straw hat."

I was having trouble making sense of this. "Jimmy's there?"

"He sure is. I was coaching him."

"Coaching him for what?"

"Well, Jimmy was telling me we needed something in the way of showmanship, now that we don't have Trooper. And he used to do dramatics when he was in school. You ought to see him, he's going to be a regular song-and-dance man, just like those fellows in vaudeville. Father Cydzik thinks so, too. Don't you, Father?"

"Your parish priest is there, too?"

"Sure. And two of the neighbors."

Not exactly the whole town, I thought, but at least some show of loyalty to Amos.

"I'm glad to hear that," I said.

"Archie Terwilliger from up the road, he's going to loan me some tools." Amos paused. I got the impression he was nodding an acknowledgment to his neighbor. "And Bill Fahey's got one of them Butler buildings he's not using."

"That's great!" A portable metal building wasn't much, compared to Amos's beautiful old barn, but at least it was a place to start.

"Darn tootin' it's great!" Amos said. "We got a lot of work to do, fixing up the stagecoach and all. Jimmy and I decided together there was no point hanging our heads and crying over spilt milk." He paused, then spoke into the distance. "Isn't that right, Jimmy?" Another pause, and Amos was talking to me again. "We're going to use the stagecoach for fund-raising, starting next weekend, raising money for the Buckeye Foundation. Jimmy says we got to do a bucket of that, even if the foundation is endowed. Well, he can explain it to you better than I can." There was yet another pause. "Jimmy says to tell you we're getting insurance right away. Look. I got to get back to what we're doing here."

"Of course." I explained that I had called to say how sorry I was that he'd lost his barn. And also that he and Jimmy were invited to supper tomorrow evening at Frannie's. "Frannie says we can make it a planning session," I said.

Amos conferred with Jimmy; both would come to supper. I hung up, feeling a renewed respect for Amos. Jimmy, too, for that matter. Even for John Philip Sousa.

$\triangledown$

# 27

On THE FLIGHT to Los Angeles I tried to imagine what I would find in Trooper's apartment. I was certain the place would be plain, functional, and painfully neat—nothing extra, nothing out of place.

When I unlocked Trooper's door I was astonished. Her computer and desk occupied an alcove just opposite the door, and letters, files, and disks littered the floor nearby. I could see through into the bedroom, where some old photos were strewn across the bed. I froze, for a brief moment afraid the place had been ransacked or, worse, that an intruder might still be present.

I listened intently, then moved slowly into the apartment. None of the furniture in the small living room had been disturbed. In the bedroom the photos strewn on the bed had apparently come from one box pulled from the closet shelf. Everything else was neat as a pin. No sign the bureau drawers had been gone through or the bathroom medicine cabinet disturbed.

I sighed with relief, and leaned back against the doorway between the kitchen and living room. Trooper must have made the mess herself, hunting for things she needed but not putting anything back.

Lady, I sent the thought, you gave me a scare.

After consulting Jimmy's list I tackled the desk and computer area first. Much of what he wanted I could pick out from the pile on the floor: computer disks labeled for various hurrahs, including "River Boat Ramble," and, of course, the one she'd started for "Gold Country Hurrah." I opened the empty suitcase I'd brought along, and put these in.

More disks held information about suppliers, customers, publicity lists, travel agents, financial records. Jimmy hadn't asked for the instruction manuals and program disks for her word processing and accounting systems, but, feeling pleased with myself, I searched those out and packed them up into the suitcase.

Also into the suitcase went Trooper's Rolodex and appointment calendar, a sheaf of recent invoices, her checkbook, and the pile of mail I had picked up at the apartment mailboxes. I added a fat, well-worn folder labeled "Travel Agents," knowing that Trooper had all her customers book through agents.

What else did we need? I found correspondence and telephone notes detailing everything Trooper had done to date on getting a private rail car for the June hurrah, as well as rate quotes from a variety of people whose services might be needed: melodrama troupes, magicians, caterers, various rental services, even a portable steam calliope.

I turned to the filing cabinet. On top was Trooper's new life insurance policy, $750,000 on the life of Mary Jane Hadley. The insurance policy's beneficiary was James D. Simpson, executive director, the Buckeye Foundation. Trooper's death had come immediately after the start-up of the foundation and the taking out of the policy, so Jimmy would no doubt soon hear from the insurance company's investigators.

I kept searching, working through the file cabinet drawers. The top one was nearly empty; apparently she'd gone through everything here. I wondered if she'd found what she'd been looking for and, for that matter, how long she'd been working on this Buckeye Foundation business. It looked to me as if all of this had gotten started quite recently. In the back of the top file cabinet drawer were her bank statements. I pulled out the twelve most recent and added them to my stash, along with file folders for her various foundations: Costa Rica Foundation, High Desert Institute,

Olympic Foundation, Friends of Fiji, and more.

I checked Trooper's answering machine. No messages. She'd left it turned off.

The file cabinet's bottom drawer held correspondence with customers. Prominent names popped out at me: politicians, socialites, entertainers, wealthy business types. I pulled out a few files, just out of curiosity. "Thank you so much for a terrific outing!" "Way to go, Troop—count me in on the next." There were also Trooper's notes on the customer's preferences and peculiarities.

I was having one last wander through the customer files, shamelessly soaking up fascinating tidbits, when I found a small section at the rear with what appeared to be Trooper's personal files. "Contents of safe deposit box." We'd need that; I pulled it out. "Volkswagen—repair records." "Insurance—condo." "Insurance—dental." We didn't need these. "Insurance—medical." "Medical records." I almost ignored these, too, but noticed the corner of a yellow form crumpled that had been hastily shoved into the file of medical records.

The crumpled page was the patient's copy of a consent form for a CT scan. There was some nearly illegible carbon-copy scribbling on it; I could make out a few words, including *subcortical*. Something to do with the brain. And the CT scan had been done in a hospital in San Diego. By all logic Trooper—who was exceedingly efficient in her use of time—would have had medical tests done at a hospital close to home. Furthermore, there was nothing else in the file.

I remembered Trooper's odd gait and, in those last few days, her uncharacteristic fatigue, and began looking around. In a wastebasket I found a tightly crumpled wad of paper. I unfolded it. There were several insurance claim forms and also a page of scribbled notes in Trooper's handwriting. The words at the top were lined out in heavy block letters: PROGRESSIVE MULTIFOCAL LEUKOENCEPHALOPATHY.

I pronounced each word carefully, especially the last, dividing it up into its components. Leuko-encephalo-pathy. *Leuko* I couldn't at the moment define. *Encephalo* had to do with the brain. *Pathy*, pathological. Not good. Especially along with the cortical something-or-other from the CT scan.

I read on, struggling to make sense out of Trooper's hurried, cramped writing. Apparently, she'd been copying information out of a medical article or reference book. "Rare neurological disease . . . rel. to immunosuppression . . . untreatable." She'd underlined that last word. "One-sided weakness . . . variable paralyses." And then a circled and exclamation-pointed word: *Dementia!* Finally, scrawled across the bottom of the page: "Fatal within months."

*Dear Lord!*

To have to face this . . . to *know*. Dementia, followed by death. No hope. No way out except the way Trooper had taken. Certainly, by her second visit to Sacramento and Buckeye, Trooper must have known how close she was to the edge. Small wonder she'd been in such a hurry to draw up papers so Jimmy could take over the hurrah and the Buckeye Foundation.

She intended to die. Frannie had been right: that's why Trooper stopped to pick flowers on that mountain road. But she'd made a big show of renting that Geo in Buckeye. She expected someone would try to kill her, I'd bet money on it.

I grabbed for the life insurance folder. What was the point of taking out an insurance policy? She had a fatal illness, which surely would be discovered when she died. No, I thought. Not if a coroner in a rural county put down the death as accidental. Or even as homicide. In a place as frugal as Tengold County, the medical examiner wouldn't go beyond the obvious causes of death.

I looked again at the forms; there was no mention of health problems. I supposed she'd been able to get past a standard medical examination, assuming she concealed the limp. Tests of her heart, lungs, and so forth would come out normal, I supposed. And she'd had that CT scan done out of town. Slowly, I smoothed the papers and put them in the file folder. I added it to the suitcase.

Why, I wondered, had Trooper merged all her foundations

and made Jimmy the benefactor—handed him the torch, so to speak? She scarcely knew him. There must be someone else, someone in her family who would have been appropriate. If she'd not had children, then there must be a niece or nephew or even a cousin she felt she could trust.

It could be that her family didn't agree with her environmental agenda, or she'd had some other kind of falling-out with them. Or maybe her family didn't want her to leave everything to her causes. Just give us our inheritance, Auntie Trooper.

How much of an inheritance was there?

I opened the suitcase and took out the bank statements. Trooper had been operating her business on the narrowest of margins. Despite some large deposits, the average monthly balance was astoundingly low, and there were charges for overdrafts. I went back to the file cabinet and pulled out the bank statements of a year ago, two years ago. They told the same story.

Trooper's international reputation, her record as an environmental philanthropist, the wealth and fame of her many clients . . . she'd managed to trade on this, charm everybody in her path, wear the aura of success like a concealing cloak, all the while leading a hand-to-mouth existence in order to support her activism.

Now I understood the rented apartment, Trooper's insistence on contracting out every possible service, her refusal to consider buying her own equipment. And now I knew why Trooper had been shamelessly mooching. She wasn't truly nasty or a flake; she desperately needed to save every dollar she could to keep her foundations going. I regretted my angry thoughts, but at the same time could not forgive her everything. She'd written a fraudulent application for life insurance. And put Jimmy in the quandary of his young life.

My time was running out; I had to be back at the airport by four o'clock. I hurriedly tidied the desk and computer station. I was almost out the door when I remembered the items scattered on the bed. I knew I'd better make time to look at them. They had been important to Trooper, or at least she'd wanted to have a last look at them.

I had no problem discovering which of the old photos was important. It was set off to one side, propped up against the pillow as if on display. It showed a twenty-years-younger Trooper standing beside another woman. Both were heavily made up. Trooper wore a sexy little-girl costume—complete with Mary Jane shoes. An interesting touch, I thought. The other woman was affecting an upper-class look, rather like a young, pouty Grace Kelly. The photo was labeled "Mary Jane and Alicia."

Alicia. I took a second, closer look. She wore pearl earrings and a pearl necklace, as well as pastel colors. Alicia Truesdale! My first, naïve conclusion was that the two were dressed for a costume party. But the overly teased hair, the heavy makeup was out of character for either of the women. Trooper had made a wild statement about having earned her start-up capital as a prostitute. . . .

This explained the uneasy exchange of glances between Trooper and Mrs. Truesdale . . . Alicia. And it also explained Mrs. T.'s eagerness to pump Vince for information—to find out if we knew. Best of all, it cast a new light on the Truesdale marriage: the ladies' man and the hooker were going to be mighty disappointed when they each learned the truth. Under all the pretense, there wasn't any money.

$\triangledown$

# 28

I FELT AS if events were moving faster than I was. It was six-thirty when I got home from the airport, and the evening at Frannie's was scheduled to start in half an hour. "Be there at seven," Frannie had admonished. "No later."

More than anything else, I wanted to sit down and go through the material I'd brought from Trooper's apartment, make notes and consider how everything fit into the overall picture. But going over Trooper's things would have to wait until my session tomorrow with Jimmy, at which time I would ask him a number of questions. For instance, how much he had known about Trooper's finances. Or her health.

I took a quick shower and changed. At precisely two minutes before seven o'clock, I presented myself at Frannie's kitchen door.

"Oh, good," she said. "You're here already. Bring those other two chairs into the dining room, will you?"

"Sure thing." The table was set with five places. "You couldn't talk Jimmy into bringing his wife and his little boy?"

"No, more's the pity. He says she's still having all-day morning sickness." Frannie busied herself rearranging things on the tabletop. "What was Trooper's apartment like?"

"Pretty much what I expected. Tiny, well organized."

"Oh, it just sounds fascinating!" Frannie always liked to glamorize everything.

I didn't want to answer Frannie's questions right now. I had too many of my own. "By the way, did Trooper ever mention her family to you?" I asked Frannie as I followed her back out into the kitchen.

"No. And I wondered about that—you know, with Jimmy being in charge of her will and all. You'd think Trooper would have had a relative do that."

"Maybe she doesn't have anybody." Trooper's career as a prostitute might have ended her family connections, I thought. At the same time I resolved not to tell anyone unless it was absolutely necessary.

"We're having baked ham and gravy with mashed potatoes," Frannie announced, "and asparagus. I've got fruit salad, too, and pecan pie. I thought Amos might like something homey. And I made a batch of my Gooey Chocolate Delights. Vince likes them."

Vince arrived first, knocking at the side door and then letting himself in. "Wow! Supper sure smells good."

Frannie beamed one of her best smiles in his direction. "It's ham. I wanted to have something you men would like."

Vince returned her smile, then began helping himself from a dish of black olives on the sideboard.

"I hope Amos and Jimmy haven't lost their way," Frannie said. She moved to the front window to have a look up and down the street.

"What did you learn in Buckeye today?" I asked Vince.

"Well, I talked to Mrs. Truesdale."

"Yes?"

"I ran into her on the main street, right outside the bank. She looked like she could use a friend, so I asked did she want to have coffee."

This was interesting. "She looked unhappy?"

"Sort of . . . well, she was scowling something fierce, but she smiled when she saw me. So I bought her a cup of coffee. And pie, too."

"They're here!" Frannie announced. "Who are you talking about?"

"Alicia Truesdale," I said. "Vince, did you find out how long they've been married?"

"No. But she couldn't have lived in Buckeye for more than about six months. She said she hadn't spent a summer here and wasn't sure she wanted to because of the heat."

"Heavens!" Frannie exclaimed. "I can understand what she means. The foothills can be *so* hot."

So she might be about to take a powder. Interesting.

Frannie greeted Amos and Jimmy effusively, taking their coats with a great deal of ceremony. Amos wore a checkered cowboy shirt that looked new, and a bolo tie. He seemed his usual courteous self. Still, he moved slowly, and, I thought, was going on sheer willpower.

"Look what I've got," Jimmy said, holding up two brochures. "Paste-ups for the gold country hurrah flyer, *and* the one for the Buckeye Foundation."

"Let's all go into the patio room," Frannie said, shooing us along. "We can spread these out on the coffee table and have a good look at them."

Jimmy unfolded the hurrah mock-up. A picture of Amos, panning for gold, graced the front page under the heading "Gold Country Hurrah," and beneath it was the typeset text of the opening sales pitch.

I picked it up and read aloud. "Stake your claim to the life of a Forty-Niner! Thrill to the excitement of panning your own gold! Six golden days of Mother Lode adventure awaits you in California's fabled foothills. You'll keep company with fandango dancers and Faro dealers, caballeros and coolies."

"Oh, my!" Frannie exclaimed. "That's wonderful!"

Jimmy grinned. "Not half-bad, is it?"

"Look," Amos said. He took the brochure from me and unfolded it. "On the inside it's got all the facts and figures."

I looked. A detailed schedule was given for each day, starting with a bus trip up Highway 49 and then the stagecoach ride into Buckeye. The inside pages also had a scenic shot of Buckeye's downtown and a photo taken of melodrama performers in costume. Two other spaces held sketches indicating what would be shown: a stagecoach and driver, a miner working at a Long Tom.

"Howie will have to reshoot those pictures," Jimmy said, suddenly serious.

I thought about the festoons of exposed film in the back of Howie's station wagon and wondered, with some foreboding, what might happen next.

"Well!" Frannie said brightly. "Let's eat."

Jimmy sought me out as we walked to the dining room. "Did you get the insurance policy?"

"That, and plenty more. I'll tell you in the morning when we have time to talk."

Jimmy nodded gravely. "I've got a lot to tell about, too. Something I found out just today. I'll bring it up in a minute."

Once we were all seated and started, Jimmy made his announcement. "The planning commission has scheduled a special meeting tomorrow night."

"On the annexation?" I asked, startled.

"Yep."

"But I thought they had to have the legal notice run in the newspaper for three weeks before they could meet to decide on that. They've got another week to go."

"They're supposed to wait," Jimmy said. "Legally, they will; they'll ratify it later. They're calling this an advisory meeting, but they'll decide everything."

"I don't understand," I said.

"We got them scared," Amos put in. "They want to hurry up and do it." He offered a wry grin. "Before any more outsiders get interested."

"And come to town to tell them how to run their business," I asked.

"Exactly," Jimmy said.

I thought about Aggie, standing staunchly outside her kitchen door and manifesting the community opinion: No outsiders wanted. But I wondered what her position would be when when the development plans went through and her place of business turned out to be in the middle of the area designated for auto dealerships. Marie's Doughnut Shop would be history. Aggie would discover that outsiders were welcome after all—at least those who could provide the city with big sales tax revenues.

"Heavens!" Frannie said. "We've only got one day to get ready to speak against the annexation."

"Some time ago, wasn't there some interest in saving the mining sites?" I asked Jimmy.

"That's right. Academics. Historical societies. Even an international expert in historical archaeology. No one paid any attention."

"Gracious! But couldn't you get them to come back?"

"Don't think so," Amos said. "Not on short notice. Besides, it didn't do any good the first time."

"In one of the newspaper articles you wrote," I said to Jimmy, "you said that construction might start within a month of approval."

He nodded glumly.

"Which might mean before June?"

Jimmy nodded again.

"Jeez," Vince moaned.

"They mean business," Amos said. "They got a lot sunk in this project, so they're not going to give up."

"Well, neither are we," Frannie said firmly.

The auto row would be the first development. Bulldozers scraping around just over the hill from the encampment wouldn't add much to the old-time ambience.

"I know what!" Frannie said. "We could get Hiram to come and testify. He went on Trooper's river hurrah, so he can tell them that the hurrah customers are rich and spend a lot of money."

"They won't pay any attention," Jimmy said. "But let's give it a try. I've got his phone number; I can give him a call."

"We need to know more about what they've done and what they plan," Frannie said, "and then we'll think of something." She looked round the table for confirmation, settling her gaze on Jimmy. "When did all this annexation business get started, anyway?"

"It was way before my time. Amos knows."

Frannie turned expectantly to Amos.

He leaned back and laced his hands behind his head. "The annexation goes way back, 1974 if I remember correctly. Yep, it was '74. That was when people first started with those environmental impact reports. They had to do one."

Maybe a look at the old report would turn up something useful, I thought.

"It was the first of those environmental reports around these parts," Amos went on. "There was plenty of irritation about it at the time."

I could well imagine. "Was McCready city manager then?"

"No. Back then he was still the local man for Consolidated. It was an important job. Tengold was one of their biggest districts."

"Was McCready into real estate investing before he set up this annexation deal?"

"Don't rightly know."

"How about now? Has he got any other deals going?" I knew the answer to that one, but I wanted to find out how close to the vest McCready played his deals.

Jimmy stirred restlessly in his chair. I signaled him to stay quiet. I wanted to discover what the general knowledge was.

"Folks say McCready and Oliver Piccard have some things going, that's the talk around town."

Again I caught Jimmy's eye. I didn't want him to mention McCready's solo deal—the real reason he'd brought Wemmer and Truesdale along on the annexation. Nobody was paying attention to the extra land to be annexed east of town; nobody knew about the community college deal.

"You know," Amos said thoughtfully, "those three have had a heck of a time hanging on to that property all these years. Even if I don't like what they're planning to do, I can see why they think they're entitled."

"What kinds of problems have they had?"

"Well, just keeping up the property taxes and all. Then last year their ship almost sunk when some outfit—they called themselves Friends of the Sierra Foothills—challenged the old environmental impact findings."

"I didn't know about that," Jimmy said.

"It was right before you came to town. These people was saying there might be chemical contamination—seepage underground."

"From what?" I asked.

"Well, up north and over the county line there was a rocket fuel plant. It was a big deal when all this aerospace stuff was new and nobody worried about pollution. But it's been a long time since those glory years. They've just about shut it down now."

"But if the rocket plant was over the county line it was on the other side of Tengold Ridge. Wouldn't pollution seep downhill, to the west?"

"I think so. But this group put up the challenge and said the Tengold Creek drainage might be polluted. The developers had to prove it wasn't."

"They had to pay for testing?"

"Yep. They had some fancy company come in and drill test holes all up and down Tengold Creek. What I heard, it cost upwards of a hundred thousand dollars."

Jimmy let out a long, low whistle.

Maybe that had something to do with Truesdale taking out a mortgage, I thought. I wondered how Wemmer and McCready stood up to their share of the costs.

"This is all very interesting," Frannie said. "But that meeting is tomorrow night. We've got to put our heads together and think of some way to stop the annexation." She got up with a resolute air and went into the kitchen; a moment later she was back with a yellow pad and a freshly sharpened pencil.

"I bought a topographical map of the Buckeye area," I said. "It's an old one and there's stuff on it I can't quite line up."

I excused myself to get the map. When I came back, Amos and Jimmy were explaining the annexation to Vince. Frannie was listening intently.

"Let's see the map," Jimmy said.

Everyone leaned forward eagerly as I spread out the topo map. "It was last updated in 1967," I said. "See, Highway 18 is these dotted lines marked Proposed Route."

"Gosh!" Amos said. "It goes way back, showing the little City Hall we had by the volunteer fire department."

"The problem I had trying to read it," I said, "was that I couldn't exactly place the new City Hall."

"Well, that's easy," Amos said. "It's right here." Frannie handed him the pencil. "Here's the road up to it. The parking lot covers this area here. And . . ."

"What does this mean here?" I asked. "The spot marked Old Cemetery."

"An old cemetery?" Jimmy leaned forward eagerly. "That might give us something."

"It was just a little cemetery," Amos said. "Don't get your hopes up. It was moved as part of the deal when the developers sold the city the land for the new City Hall and for an expansion of the corporation yard." He glanced up at me. "I forgot to tell you about that. Anyhow," he went on, "it was real small, maybe ten or twelve graves. They moved them all over to the main cemetery."

"Did the developers have to pay for that?" Jimmy asked.

"Nope. They took it out of redevelopment funds." Amos shrugged. "McCready said it was legal."

"Show me where the mining sites are," I said to Amos.

"All right." He picked up the pencil again and began marking the map. "There was ditches here. They brought water in to mine the creek. And way over here is the ground sluicing—what we used to call the Chinese Diggings."

"And it was these diggings that brought on all the attention?"

"Yep. For a while."

"And over here. This hillside is where the Chinese rockers were used?"

"Right."

"Then what's over on this other hillside? I saw some rounded humps there, but I didn't think they were Chinese rocker mounds."

"You've got a good eye," Amos said. "They aren't. That's the old Chinese burial ground."

"What!" Jimmy exclaimed.

"Hardly nobody knows about it," Amos said. "Back a hundred years ago they buried the coolies here. On top of each burial mound was a brick with the name of their village in China. The idea was that when times was better, they'd send them back. Their religion called for it."

"Oh, my," Frannie said. "How sad. They never got to go home?"

"Nope. In fact, there used to be another burial ground just like it, way up on the other side of Tengold Creek. It's been gone for years; the ground was dredged."

Frannie's eyes flew wide open; she put a hand to her mouth. "Why, that's terrible!"

"Well, you got to understand how folks felt about Chinamen in the old days. Like they weren't quite people, and their burial place didn't count as a *real* cemetery."

"That's just terrible," Frannie repeated.

"You're right, Frannie," I said. "It was terrible—unthinking and racist. But now the remaining Chinese burial ground is going to be very useful."

"You got it!" Jimmy exclaimed. "We have a cemetery . . . located . . ." He consulted the map. "Right in the middle of the proposed discount mall."

▽

# 29

JIMMY AND I had agreed to meet the next day at Amos's. This bothered me; I'd wanted some time alone to talk with him.

When I arrived, Amos and Jimmy already had their heads together at Amos's kitchen table and were busily outlining points to be made at tonight's Buckeye Planning Commission meeting.

"Here's our thinking so far," Jimmy told me. "Number one, Amos makes a pitch for the historic value of the mining sites."

"Will he mention the Chinese burials?"

"No. We're going to sandbag on that, pull it at the last minute. But we want Amos to make his pitch—tell about the sites in detail—so it's all written down in the record."

"Okay, fair enough."

"Right. Number two, Hiram does his bit—talks about how much money is involved in one of these hurrahs. He'll give 'em dope on the River Boat Ramble, and then submit a projected spending sheet I've made up for the hurrah here."

"Have you really got anything convincing?" I asked. There wasn't much in town to sell to tourists—gold pans at the hardware store, maybe, and at the pharmacy the usual coffee mugs and knickknacks. Plus gas at the gas station. The rich folks wouldn't lunch at Aggie's establishment, or go down to the Yellow Lantern.

"There's more local spending than you'd think," Jimmy said. "Most of it is support for the providers. We'd book a block of rooms at the riding academy for the melodrama players, the caterer's people, and the crew that puts up the tents. The caterer will buy some of the provisions locally, or at least that's what I'm going to put down. And I'll put down they'll use local kids for the unskilled labor."

"Okay," I said. "So far so good."

"Then when Hiram's finished with the money part I come on representing the Buckeye Foundation." He grinned. "I'm going to maunder on about the diminishing stockpile of authentic placer mining sites, the uniqueness of the Chinese Diggings as evidenced by international scholastic interest . . ." He waved an arm expansively. "Et cetera, et cetera."

"Don't get too carried away," I said. "They might cut you off before you can drop your bombshell."

Amos looked worried. "They could do that, all right," he cautioned Jimmy.

"Okay." Jimmy straightened in his chair. "I'll limit myself to a few well-chosen remarks for the record, then cut to the bombshell drop."

I tried to imagine what would happen next. "Who'll be chairing the meeting? Not McCready."

"No," Jimmy told me. "It'll be the planning commission chairman, the right honorable Oliver Piccard."

I might have known. "How do you think he'll react?"

Jimmy looked thoughtful. He'd been so busy savoring his moment of triumph that he'd not considered what might happen next. "He'll really be surprised, I guess," Jimmy said.

Amos stirred in his chair. "Him being a newcomer to Buckeye, I doubt he even knows the Chinese used to bury their dead that way. It's a shame. Most folks around here never give those mounds a second thought."

"So it's a total surprise to Piccard," I said. "Still, he'll see the implications right away. And McCready even quicker, no doubt."

Both Amos and Jimmy nodded their agreement.

"So they're stuck," I went on. "They can't go ahead with the annexation without making allowances for the Chinese burial ground as a cemetery *and* as a historic site."

"If I know those three," Jimmy said, "they'll ask to have the meeting continued right away, without one further word in public about those gravesites. They'll want to sort out the options among themselves. Maybe they'll decide to amend the land-use plan to allow for the cemetery."

"But a cemetery isn't the most desirable accoutrement to a discount mall," I pointed out.

"Maybe they'll offer to have it moved," Amos said, "like the other cemetery."

"They're going to be out a bundle if they have to do that," I said. I tried to visualize the long, sloping hillside with its haphazard rows of mounds. "How many graves do you think there are out on that hillside?" I asked Amos.

"A hundred, maybe. Maybe more."

Jimmy was jubilant. "Great stuff! An even bigger monkey wrench than the pollution scare!"

I was suddenly struck with the view from the other side. The developers would see this as yet another delay before they could start getting their money back out of the real estate deal. Worse, someone among them had felt threatened enough by Trooper's interference to kill her. And now that person would feel even more threatened.

▽

# 30

Moments before the planning commission meeting was to begin, Vince squeezed in to sit beside me in the back row.

"Where've you been all this time?" I whispered.

"Checking into some stuff." Vince was obviously pleased with himself.

"And . . . ?"

"Well, first off, I tracked down that forestry department investigator like you asked me to—took half the afternoon, but it was worth it."

"Come on, Vince," I said. "Give! The meeting's about to start." Oliver Piccard—wavy hair, slouched posture, pasty skin, and all—was leading the planning commissioners in to sit at the front of the room.

Vince leaned close. "That gas can from the barn fire," he said. "They found a real clear print on the bottom."

"Have they identified whose print it is?"

"No, but they will. They got to. I told the CDF guy it would be Wemmer's mechanic, Kelly."

"Good for you," I whispered. "Does Palooka know about the print?"

"I told him. He looked awful down in the mouth about it, too."

By now I was certain Kelly was our man for the "Don't tread on me" stuff. But someone else had put him up to it, and had shot Trooper, because Kelly was at work then.

The planning commissioners were now all in their places, shuffling their papers and checking their individual microphones. The table at which they sat was on a raised dais. Beside it was a podium with a spare microphone, presumably for citizens and others to make presentations, and beside that a table with yet another microphone, occupied by Mc-Cready and a stenographer. A second table had been crowded in as well, at which sat Wemmer and Truesdale. And the audience was separated from the dignitaries by a rail—very much, I thought, like the communion rail in a cathedral.

Considering the nature of the event, the audience was small. Twenty people, perhaps. Jimmy and Amos sat in the front row, alongside them Frannie and Hiram. Frannie, eager to protest any threat to the Chinese gravesites, had made certain she'd be in time to sit up front. I'd stayed in the back, waiting for Vince.

Piccard opened the meeting and read a legal description of the proposed annexation. As he droned away at it I decided this was a deliberate tactic: Make the thing so dull nobody would pay attention.

Vince nudged me. "Aren't you going to ask me what else I found out?" he whispered.

"Sure. What did you learn?"

"My buddy on the Fairville police force finally came through. I got detailed stuff on the finances of our three developers."

"Great!"

"Okay," Vince went on, sotto voce. "Now with Mc-Cready . . ." He pulled out his notebook.

A man in front of us turned and glared at us, finger to lips in a shushing gesture.

Vince and I lapsed into silence. Piccard droned on. I leaned to the side a little, catching sight of Jimmy's face in quarter-profile. He looked tense, with no trace of the jubilation he'd displayed earlier.

This afternoon I'd at last had a chance to confront him about the insurance policy. He'd known about Trooper's health, but had not known how little time she had left.

"If we keep quiet it's a felony," I'd told him, "conspiring to defraud an insurance company."

"I suppose so." His words were nearly inaudible.

"When did she tell you about it?"

"The day she went over to Leona to get all that legal work done. She told me first."

Trooper's usual modus operandi, I thought. She hadn't given him time to consider what he was getting into—just laid the news on him and expected him to say yes.

Jimmy took a long, deep breath, something like a sigh in reverse. "She told me about that disease, I mean what it was going to do to her. And that she had to have somebody to carry on. And then she told me about the money, not really having any, I mean. She said people just thought she did, and it always worked."

I remembered something Trooper had come up with once, at Frannie's. "It's the perception that counts." She'd used her Mae West voice, accompanied by an expert wiggle of her shoulder.

"I bet she told you to just keep up a front and the money would come in somehow."

Jimmy looked up at me, startled. "That's pretty much what she said."

"It's the perception that counts." I spoke more to myself than to him.

"That's exactly what she said," Jimmy exclaimed, "just before she left to go to Leona."

"She said it to me once, too. Only I didn't really understand what she meant."

We fell into silence, each thinking our own thoughts.

I was the one who brought us back to the problem at hand. "We have a noble cause, but we're still dealing with fraud," I said.

Jimmy asked me to stay quiet about the insurance, but only until he could do enough fund-raising to recoup money he'd invested in the project. "Don't tell my wife," he begged. "I took money out of savings and told her it was from the foundation. Just give me a few weeks. I know I can do it. Maybe the Buckeye Foundation will be solvent enough to pay me. Or even to keep going permanently." His eyes shone with excitement. "Golly, that's what I want."

He had a vision for the glorious good the Buckeye Foundation could do—and maybe would. Still, I had a knotty problem in ethics, but had ended up promising to keep silent temporarily.

Piccard finally came to the end of his description of the annexation. The bulk of the verbiage had been spent on the plans of the three developers, with only the briefest description of the large tract to the east. And no mention, of course, of the community college district's plans, or that McCready was standing by to make himself a multimillionaire when he developed the housing tract.

Amos stirred restlessly in his seat. His turn was coming up, I thought, his time to explain his beloved mining sites.

But Piccard called on McCready first, to give estimates of tax revenues from the auto sales park and the discount mall. McCready, in his role as city manager, stepped up behind the commissioner's table and pinned a large chart to the wall. It showed anticipated sales tax revenues over the next five years—an astoundingly optimistic projection, it seemed to me.

McCready began to explain it, making no mention of the downside risk—for instance, that Wemmer might build his big fancy emporium and find himself with no more sales than in previous years, and a lot of new expenses to boot. There was no mention of the proposed electronic sign.

Wemmer sat at his table on the other side of the rail separating audience and officials, grinning and nodding as McCready went on about the projected tax revenues. Even sitting, I thought, Wemmer seemed to strut.

How could Wemmer do what he was doing? His family had lived in these parts for generations. Wemmers must have driven horses and wagons up present-day Buckeye Boulevard to shop in town for decades, heading home with sacks of flour and bolts of cloth and tools for the Wemmer homestead. Wemmer children must have skipped down the rural road that Highway 18 once had been on their way to Nye schoolhouse. And, as a child, Wemmer had undoubtedly played on the grassy slopes where the huge sign would plant its feet—climbed the old oak trees, played hide-and-seek behind the boulders. Now he was ready to throw it all away, transform his hometown into yet another cookie-cutter nowhere.

When at last McCready finished with the tax projections, Piccard—with manifest distaste—announced that Mr. Amos Fugaldi, Mr. Hiram Cohen, and Mr. James Simpson had requested opportunities to speak.

I nudged Vince. "Let me see your notebook," I whispered.

Vince obligingly dug it out. I looked through the pages. There were notes about his conversation with the CDF investigator, then came a section he'd labeled "Financial."

The first part dealt with McCready. His salary from the city was small, his retirement from Consolidated generous. He owned his home free and clear, the same for his Chrysler. He paid real estate taxes on a large number of parcels; there was also a long list of CD accounts. I watched him as he listened to Amos, an almost-concealed smirk playing around his mouth. I knew what motivated him. He loved what he did: conniving, manipulating, earning ever more wealth. He'd do it no matter how much money he had. I'd read somewhere that men like McCready confuse wealth and worth; it sounded true enough to me.

Amos made a good job of his presentation, ending it with a prepared statement. We'd all worked on what to say, but tried to leave it in Amos's words.

"Mining sites aren't all of what we've got here; we've got a lot of atmosphere. We need to keep Buckeye pretty much the way it is. Our town can have a good future without big-city development. All we have to do is encourage people to come and enjoy the old-time things they aren't hardly going to find anywhere else." Amos paused, looked directly at Wemmer, Truesdale, and McCready. "That way we can save the old things—things that can never be replaced—for our children and grandchildren."

McCready put his hand up in front of his face, yawning.

Wemmer stirred impatiently. Truesdale stared straight ahead, affecting a style as bored as McCready's.

Hiram was next up. He faltered several times getting started, but then cleared his throat and began to speak firmly. He told of the average numbers of people on a Hadley hurrah, the profits made, the money spread around local communities.

Satisfied he was on his way to making a good presentation, I went back to Vince's notebook to check on Wemmer's finances. There was a lot of Wemmer property in and around Buckeye, all of it owned free and clear—the car sales lot being the largest of these tracts. Much of the rest of it had been split up when the right-of-way for Highway 18 was purchased. He had some money invested, too, but nowhere near as much as McCready, although his bill-paying record was far less tidy due to some disruptions at the time of his divorce. And his auto and truck business seemed to be faring well enough.

When Hiram concluded his speech and had distributed expense and outlay sheets for the June hurrah, Jimmy was up. Bomb-dropping time.

Jimmy came on with considerable aplomb, introducing himself as executive director of the Buckeye Foundation. He explained that the new organization, headquartered in Buckeye, had become an umbrella organization for all the other foundations established by Trooper Hadley. "I'm sure some of you will be surprised at the news, but this little town has now become a nerve center for the preservation of historic sites and natural resources throughout the world."

It was good stuff; he'd rehearsed a lot. As far as I was concerned, he was ready for presentations to wealthy prospective donors. I could imagine him going through the points with a well-prepared flip-chart or perhaps a slide presentation.

I was about to turn my attention back to Vince's notebook when Jimmy started in on the need to preserve local historic attractions. He skillfully described local historic sites, working his way around to the Oriental miners who'd toiled at the Chinese Diggings. He extolled their sense of community, their determination to preserve their own culture and observe the requirements of their religion. And then he dropped the bomb: There were a hundred or more nineteenth-century Chinese graves on a hillside at the center of the proposed discount mall.

Instantly, both Piccard and Wemmer wore *huh!* expressions. Truesdale stared straight ahead, his mouth slowly opening, his skin growing paler and paler until it showed an almost greenish pallor. McCready, smooth as always, stood. "If the honorable chairman would grant me a few moments . . ."

By now the audience had begun to stir; people, obviously astonished, turned to each other and began to talk. I wondered if they were surprised the graves were there, or merely that somebody had declared they must be taken seriously. McCready gestured impatiently at Piccard, indicating he should use his gavel. Piccard, after a moment, brought the gavel down smartly and called for order.

"If you would grant me a few moments, Mr. Piccard," McCready said, "I would like to present my advice. Acting in lieu of our city council, who are not present at this meeting, I suggest we need clarification as to the status of these alleged gravesites before proceeding further."

The audience was buzzing again. McCready made another impatient gesture to Piccard, who once more gaveled the meeting to order.

"Therefore," McCready continued, "considering the possibility that these graves are not a cemetery by conventional standards . . ." he paused to take a deep breath, "and the certainty they cannot be considered an indigenous burial ground, we need legal advice—a clarification of the status of this . . . um . . . site. Mr. Chairman, I counsel you that this meeting be adjourned and the subject matter carried over to another time."

Piccard, his pasty face rapidly turning ruddy, banged the gavel yet again. "Meeting adjourned," he declared. "This meeting is continued to a future date."

$\bigtriangledown$

# 31

I HELD OUT the notebook for Vince to take back. We were sitting in his car, still in the parking lot outside City Hall. Hiram and Frannie had left for Sacramento and Amos and Jimmy had gone to Amos's place to work on plans for the hurrah—the fuss and delay over the Chinese burial sites would, if nothing else, give us enough time to go ahead with a hurrah sans development activities.

The information in Vince's notebook revealed that Truesdale was broke, desperately broke. His bank accounts were at zilch, and credit card charges and other bills had piled up. He was behind on his home mortgage payments and payments on the Toyota as well. It was a wonder the car hadn't been repossessed.

"Truesdale's the one," I said. "I should have realized sooner."

"Aw, you couldn't have known."

"Yes, I could have," I persisted. "For instance, he was anxious to lease the ground for the hurrah, cash on the barrelhead, ready to go for it no matter what the others wanted to do. And when you encountered Alicia Truesdale outside the bank, she must have just learned there was no money." I paused for a moment's thought. "So by now Truesdale must know he didn't marry a wealthy woman— just a fortune hunter like himself."

"Aw . . . she's a nice lady. She was awful nice to me."

"Then I hope she's already packed her suitcases and left

town. Truesdale's a killer. He has to have been the one who shot Trooper."

"How do you know?" Vince asked.

"More than likely McCready and Wemmer were where someone saw them that afternoon. We know Kelly was at work. And Truesdale is a marksman, a member of the rod and gun club over in Leona."

"Yeah. But that's all circumstantial. Besides, how did he know she was going up there?"

That had me stumped. McCready could easily know because Kelly would tell Palooka and Palooka would pass the information along to his boss. Wemmer would know she rented the vehicle from his establishment. But Truesdale—how could a retired chiropractor, staying at home, know Trooper's movements?

Staying at home . . . of course!

"All Truesdale had to do was look out his window," I said. "I bet you can see all up and down Highway 18."

"Jeez . . . you're right. He could keep track of everything."

"Truesdale's our man."

"Yeah. Only one problem. We can't prove it."

"How about the shell casings you found?"

"Can't prove nothing. I found two sets of casings, and one set didn't have any prints. Most people leave prints on the casings when they load a rifle, so these was from our killer. He probably wore gloves."

Truesdale was a chiropractor; he might easily have had latex gloves around.

"Wouldn't there be rifling marks on the bullets that killed Trooper?"

"There would be. But the sheriff's guys said finding a match was a needle-in-the-haystack proposition."

"They knew it might be one of the three developers?"

"I tried to tell 'em. They didn't want to hear it."

"I can imagine."

"They gotta listen now. We got some good circumstantial

stuff on Truesdale. Except . . ." He heaved a sigh. "Except if he was smart enough to keep his prints off the casings, he's probably ditched the rifle by now."

"Or sold it to someone. That would take care of an incriminating piece of evidence and bring him some cash."

"Yeah. Sheesh! You'd have to check every deer hunter in the county, and you still might not find the guy he sold it to."

So much for that line of inquiry.

I put my mind to the Kelly-Truesdale relationship. I had trouble with the image of Truesdale, dapper and polite, hanging out with the grubby Kelly—fanning his prejudices, urging him to rail against Trooper, giving him go-ahead signals to act on whatever violent impulses he had.

"I just can't imagine Truesdale talking Kelly into what he did. You know, saying things to get him into the mood, using that kind of language and all."

"Aw, Emma, you don't know Truesdale."

"What do you mean?"

"That guy's real different when women aren't around. He talks dirty, awful dirty."

Bingo! Truesdale was a closet foul-mouth.

Now I could imagine the right words coming from him, imprecations against women, crude anatomical language, accusations that would feed Kelly's hostility and anger, putting together Trooper's femaleness with the fact that she was an outsider. A *meddling* outsider.

"Do you suppose Truesdale drew the snake picture?" I asked Vince.

He was thoughtful. "I dunno. It don't really matter unless we can prove something."

We sat for a time in companionable silence—shared dejection, I thought, a mutual sense of futility. I put my mind back on the problem of the notes, of finding proof, and was suddenly struck with the obvious. "There have to be more notes somewhere," I said.

"Huh? Oh, I getcha. Like if they was going to do something more, they'd have to have one to leave."

"There has to be the original, too."

"Right!" Vince sat up straight in his seat.

"I'll bet Truesdale keeps the master," I said, growing excited. "And Kelly's got the extra copies."

"Jeez! If we could just catch 'em with those snake notes. Both of them."

"Truesdale in particular."

"Search warrants," Vince said. "We got to get search warrants . . . tonight!"

"You're right," I said. "With everything that's happened, they might get nervous and get rid of the warning notes."

"We gotta go up to the Tengold sheriff's office for the search warrants. Start there and then talk to a judge, convince him we got probable cause in a serious case—that maybe Kelly's gonna do something again, or Truesdale's gonna fly the coop." He started his car's engine.

"Wait a minute! You don't need me along." It might be morning before Vince got the warrants. I wanted to check on Truesdale's and Kelly's whereabouts.

"Aw, I can't leave you here. It's late."

"Not that late. The planning commission meeting broke up before nine o'clock." I glanced at the clock on his dash. "It isn't even ten yet."

"What do you got to stay here for? You could go over to Leona with me."

"Vince, I *want* to stay here. It's the best idea, really. I can keep an eye on things."

At last Vince departed, having first dropped me back at my truck. As soon as he left I headed for the doughnut shop, the only spot in town still open other than the Yellow Lantern.

Aggie grudgingly provided me with a cup of stale coffee. And I'd no sooner settled down at the first table outside the door than Palooka's car pulled into the parking lot. I watched as he made his way down the row of outdoor tables, a folded magazine under one arm.

"Good evening," I said when he came abreast of me. He nodded curtly but said nothing. He soon emerged from

Aggie's with coffee and the inevitable bag of doughnuts. He sat down at his usual table, steadfastly ignoring me.

How much did he know? Surely he knew Kelly was involved. But did he know who put Kelly up to it? I studied him, watching as he began munching his way through the doughnuts: bite, chew, swallow. Another doughnut. Maybe he didn't know, but suspected what was going on and was trying to keep his friend out of trouble. Or maybe he knew everything. Bite, chew, swallow. There was no way of reading the man.

I considered where we might find copies of the "Don't tread on me" note. If Truesdale had the original in his possession it would probably be in his house. No, more likely his car; he wouldn't have wanted his wife to find it.

I looked at my watch. Not even half past ten. Vince probably was just arriving in Leona. But what if he couldn't get the warrants? And what if our suspects destroyed the evidence while I sat here fiddling with my coffee cup?

Palooka wadded up his doughnut bag and rose ponderously to his feet. He deposited the trash in an outside container, walked by me without a word or gesture, and wedged himself into the police car. I stared after its departing red taillights. They jounced down Buckeye Boulevard, then receded as the car headed east on Highway 18.

I went back to the "Don't tread on me" notes. What I most wanted to do was catch Truesdale with one in his possession. But searching his house—at least now—was out of the question. Lights shone brightly there; the man was still up.

Kelly was another matter.

I crumpled my Styrofoam coffee cup and hurried to deposit it in the trash. I waved cheerily to Aggie. She ignored me.

I went to my truck, my mind already filling with the details of the enterprise ahead. The first stop would be the Yellow Lantern. I had a hunch I'd see Kelly there, which would leave the coast clear for me to search his living quarters—he not only worked at Wemmer's but also lived there.

I spotted the ratty pickup that I knew was Kelly's in the Yellow Lantern parking lot. Just to be sure I went to the bar entrance, opening the door a few inches. Kelly was in clear view, sitting at a table that had an electronic game embedded in its surface. As I watched he signaled the bartender for another beer.

My lucky night. I wouldn't be gathering evidence illegally, I thought, but merely locating it. When Vince came back with the sheriff and the search warrants we'd know exactly where to look.

I drove back down the highway. Everything seemed in order at the Wemmer agency. I could see night lights in the sales hut and the service bay; a fainter light shone in the building at the rear that housed the main shop and Kelly's living quarters. I continued until I was beyond the agency, then pulled over and parked my truck on the highway shoulder. I took my flashlight, as much for self-defense as illumination, and started walking.

So far so good, I thought. I walked steadily in the darkness, contemplating the places I might search—assuming I could get in. If the notes weren't in Kelly's living quarters, they were probably in his toolbox in the shop. Or in his truck, but I'd have to wait to check that.

When I reached the agency I dodged pools of glare from the sales hut and the service bay, and moved to the far side of a row of parked cars, positioning myself for a stealthy approach to the repair shop. I stopped twice, certain each time I heard someone following me. Nonsense! There'd be no one here this time of night. Still, each time I thought I heard a suspicious sound I retreated farther into the safety of the darkness—waiting, circling around, watching. Each time I could find no one skulking behind me.

At the main shop I went around to the back and looked in through a window. I saw two racks for hoisting cars, as well as the usual array of equipment. At the far end was a small office and behind it a rest room. Kelly's living quarters had to be at that end of the building—the plumbing for the rest room and his bathroom would be back to back.

I moved along the wall and around the back, groping my way in near-complete darkness. Just before I came to the far corner, my searching fingers enountered what I'd been looking for, the doorway to Kelly's place. I turned the knob; it was unlocked.

Inside, a smell of cigarettes and stale beer assailed me. My flashlight revealed an overstuffed chair with torn upholstery, empty beer cans overflowing a cardboard box beside it. I also saw an unmade bed, a chest of drawers, and a closed door— either the closet or the bathroom.

It was a closet. A scant array of clothes, mostly work shirts and pants, hung among a tangle of clothes hangers. There was also a suit, still in its cleaner's bag, and a cheap, fancy cowboy shirt. A pair of work boots were on the floor, as well as a scuffed pair of moccasins and several mismatched dirty socks. Above was a shelf, with a pair of worn dress shoes, quite dusty, and an old suitcase.

I pulled the suitcase down and went through the contents. A high school yearbook. Old report cards. Canceled checks. A framed photograph, obviously of his mother—she had the same surly look, the same lank hair. A few letters. A key, apparently to the suitcase, and the torn stub of a movie ticket from a theater in Leona.

I put the suitcase back and looked through the dresser drawers. Nothing. No incriminating "Don't tread on me" notes among the socks and underwear, the comic books, and girlie magazines. I checked behind the dresser mirror, even under the bed. Still nothing.

I moved on to the tiny bathroom. Squeezed toothpaste tubes. An overflowing wastebasket. Old pill bottles. And, beside the toilet, more girlie magazines. I gave up on finding the notes here.

Back outside, I again groped my way along the back wall of the repair shop. Gathering my courage, I walked boldly across the well-lit front of the shop and tried the pedestrian door that was beside the roll-up doors to the two hoist areas. Again, no luck.

The notes weren't in Kelly's room, so the likeliest places were his toolbox or his truck. I imagined his toolbox in the shop, on the workbench. The image taunted me. As if with X-ray vision, my mind's eye could see inside. And, at the very bottom, I imagined a stack of the notes. The image was compellingly vivid.

There was still the service bay. I was determined to check it, despite my conviction that the notes were in the shop. Staying away from the spill-out of light from it, I approached the bay from the back side. There was one small window, high up. No possibilities here. I made my way along the side, heading for the front and keeping to the shadows. The front was protected by a pull-across metal grille, fastened on the side near me with a padlock as big as my fist. I tested it and discovered it had been closed but not locked. Kelly's doing, I surmised, smiling to myself in the dark.

There wasn't much in the bay. Signs. Tires on flat carts, to be wheeled outside during the day. A stack of batteries. And gasoline cans, just like the one left at Amos's barn.

I felt my way along the back wall. A workbench ran the length of it, with cupboards below and above. Unwilling to use my flashlight in the open-fronted bay, I felt my way across the work surface and through each cabinet, bumping my fingers against unexpected tools, encountering numerous small objects I couldn't identify, and one I could—a dead mouse. There were two more cupboards. I persevered; they held only neatly stacked cans of oil.

Once outside I hurried to the privacy of the shadows, then moved toward the highway. Once on the road, I put the last reaches of light from the Wemmer lot behind me as quickly as I could. And even after I'd reached the safety of darkness I kept up a brisk pace, eager for the familiar security of my truck.

I was within thirty paces of it when I heard a sound behind me. I started to turn, but wasn't quick enough. A hand pulled against my forehead. At the same time another hand was planted firmly at the back of my neck. The pressure was astoundingly painful; I made no struggle.

"You're a smart bitch."

Truesdale's voice.

"A damn smart bitch, to value your neck as you do."

"You're hurting me."

"That's the point. I want you to follow my instructions."

"You shot Trooper."

"Shut your mouth, cunt!"

The pressure increased. And the pain.

"We're going to walk together, old cunt, back to your truck."

Obediently, I started moving. I waited awhile before I spoke again. "Don't tell me, let me guess," I said, struggling for a light tone. "I'm going to take a ride and then have an accident."

"Exactly. Nothing original, but I can carry it off."

"You don't have to," I said. "No one can prove you did it—killed Trooper, I mean."

"Ah, yes, but you know."

"If you kill me it won't change the situation with the annexation. It's still going to be delayed."

"But I'll have the satisfaction." His voice was harsh, vindictive. "Bitches. You and Alicia and that Hadley broad. You've wrecked me financially."

"You give us credit for more power than we've got."

The response was a sudden tightening of his grip; the pain was intense.

"I'll do whatever you say," I said quickly.

"Damn right you will." He giggled, a dry mirthless sound. "You know, with the hold I've got on you—forehead in the left hand, fifth cervical vertebra in the right—I could snap your neck just like that. Kill you instantly. Trust me." Again, the giggle. "Trust me, I'm a doctor."

I could make out the outline of my truck in the darkness ahead. We stopped moving when we were a few feet behind it.

"You're going to open the door on the driver's side," Truesdale said, "slowly and carefully."

A few more moments and he'd snap my neck, then push

my body across the seat of the truck. His hand was hard and cold on my forehead; the pressure at the back of my neck was vicious. I was controlled entirely. No choice. No way out.

Car lights flashed on from a car parked in front of my truck. Truesdale jerked me around, coming near to snapping my neck on the spot.

I squinted at the dark form of the car behind the headlights. It was a police car—Palooka's. He emerged from it with astounding speed and stood regarding me and Truesdale from behind the shelter of the open car door.

"Hello, there," Truesdale said inanely. At the same time he moved swiftly—too swiftly to give me a chance to respond—dropping his hand from my forehead and capturing both my arms behind my back. I found myself in another painful position.

"You've seen this lady around town, haven't you?" Truesdale called to Palooka. "Well, whether you know it or not, she's nuttier than a fruitcake—tells wild stories. I found her on private property, acting strange. It's lucky I spotted her."

Fancy footwork on Truesdale's part, but a flimsy story.

"Damn lucky for you I spotted her," Truesdale went on. "I was fixing to take her over to the psych ward at Leona, save you the trouble. Citizen's arrest."

Palooka nodded gravely as if in assent with Truesdale's wild statements. My God! Was he going to go along with this line of malarkey? But then, maybe Truesdale didn't need a story that made sense. Maybe any old story would do—goodbuddy Palooka would follow along.

"Yes, sir," Truesdale continued. "Citizen's arrest. Going to save you a lot of trouble."

His hold on my arms shifted slightly; he was getting ready to do something different. It was now or never. I wrenched free, pulled away. Truesdale, caught by surprise, lunged at me. Taking advantage of his momentum, I shoved him with all the force I could muster, straight toward Palooka.

Palooka, in a boxer's automatic reaction, decked the man.

⬇

# 32

THE HOT MAY sunshine drenched the area behind City Hall.
I was astounded at the scene before me, not having expected
so much of a transformation. Frannie, acting as volunteer social director for the Buckeye Foundation, had seemingly waved
a magic wand for Buckeye Appreciation Day.

She'd arranged for a huge caterer's tent so white it sparkled. Its side walls were furled to admit the random breezes;
pennants flew from the top. A pathway of gold indoor-out-
door carpeting led up to it, both pathway and tent bordered
with huge potted hydrangeas in an array of pinks and blues.
Inside the tent were bright balloons and hanging baskets
filled with red and coral begonias.

Jimmy's fund-raising had brought in surprising amounts
during the past few weeks—it was an absolute pleasure to
come back from the post office with a sack of mail, then open
the envelopes filled with checks and credit card pledges. We'd
long since forgone the insurance money. Still, I'd had no idea
the Buckeye Foundation could afford such an extravagant
display.

The caterer's assistants were everywhere, young men and
women in slim black pants and gold cummerbunds dispensing
champagne and hors d'oeuvres. Among them strolled Vince,
looking well tailored in a security guard outfit Frannie had
selected for him, and, I suspected, had paid a pretty penny to
have altered. Frannie herself, perspiring greatly but nonetheless looking elegant in an apricot linen dress and a ribbon-
bedecked straw hat, bustled happily among the crowd.

Not far from the caterer's tent was a smaller one, Buckeye Foundation headquarters for the day. A table within was overflowing with a huge floral arrangement sent by Jimmy's mother, and Jimmy was busily handing out gold country hurrah brochures and Buckeye Foundation fund-raising leaflets. Hiram's beautiful old Lincoln, again resplendent after two months of intensive work, graced the area adjoining the Buckeye Foundation tent and was surrounded by a crowd of admirers.

Amos had set up a gold panning demonstration and had put up his Long Tom equipment, and the stagecoach beside it. A sign indicated when demonstrations and rides were scheduled. Amos, in his straw hat and red bandana, chatted with passersby, while Howie happily took photos. I noticed quite a few Buckeye residents among the crowd—not all convinced, maybe, but at least curious.

In all, the changes since March were considerable.

Kelly, incriminated by both the gasoline-can fingerprint and "Don't tread on me" notes, found just as I'd suspected in his toolbox, had no money for bail. He'd languished in the lock-up over at Leona until Palooka had intervened, gotten his childhood friend out on his own recognizance, and helped him find work in a nearby town.

Palooka had been very angry at Truesdale for taking advantage of Kelly. In fact, the night he'd rescued me, he'd been keeping an eye on him. He'd hoped events at the planning commission meeting would set the good doctor to doing something incriminating, and had followed him when he set out to waylay me.

Truesdale at first had stuck to his ludicrous story that I was mentally unbalanced, and later tried to claim Kelly had lied about their association. But the pretense ended when the master copy of the "Don't tread on me" note was found in his garage.

McCready stepped into the act then, going Truesdale's bail and later buying out his share in the annexation project. Truesdale was free until his case came up—he'd left town in

a hurry. I imagined he was at this very moment plying his
Arthur Murray charm somewhere, trolling for rich widows.

Jimmy signaled, indicating he wanted me to take over at
the Buckeye Foundation booth.

"McCready's waiting to talk to me about these," he said
as I took a seat in the booth. He waved a sheaf of literature
from land conservancy organizations. "He wants to know
about tax advantages for signing a conservation easement."

I wished Jimmy luck. Maybe McCready would change his
plans, now that land right in the middle of his discount mall
couldn't be developed. The hillside filled with nineteenth-
century Chinese burials—the adjacent mining sites, too—
might become what Jimmy called a historic island in the
middle of town. He'd worked hard to sell the idea; we
could hope.

Palooka joined me at the Buckeye booth. He wasn't in his
policeman's uniform, but in white duck pants and a white
shirt. The outfit was in perfect taste, but still gave him some-
what the appearance of a young whale. His air of dignity
precluded laughter, however, and I noticed that his belt now
fastened several notches shorter than formerly.

"I've got something to show you," he said. He displayed
a much-thumbed magazine. "Back issue, from the library."

Now what? Palooka and I had had some interesting conversations on topics he'd come up with in his extensive reading—the ecology of the Galápagos Islands, the construction
of the first subway tubes under New York City, the possible
harm done by electromagnetic force fields. Palooka had a
wide-ranging and curious intellect.

He thumbed through the magazine pages, then folded one
back. "Here, look at this." It was an article about the Chinese archaeologist who had some years back discovered a
legion of terra-cotta soldiers at an ancient burial site. "He's
the guy who dug up that whole clay army in China. He was
here in Buckeye once, did you know that?"

"Right. He was interested in the Chinese Diggings."

"He's coming back to look at the burial sites."

"Good!" I said. "Maybe now the locals will begin to believe us when we say those sites are important."

Palooka sighed. "And maybe people won't."

"Well," I said. "It might not be a good idea to wish too hard that Buckeye become a tourist attraction."

"What do you mean?"

"There's an old saying. Something to the effect that you have to be careful what you wish for because you might get it."

He gave me a quizzical look.

"You know where they have the gold pan display at the hardware store?"

"Yeah."

"I was by there this morning. They've added a whole new line of tacky souvenirs."

"Oh." He grinned. "I getcha."

"Things do have to change, I suppose. And better the Invasion of the Tacky Monster than the obliteration of the landscape."

He nodded his agreement.

"I've got more news," I said. "The Buckeye Foundation is going to challenge the use of redevelopment funds for that electronic sign for the car sales lots."

"I heard the same thing." Palooka looked thoughtful. "McCready might give up on that."

"Especially if the Buckeye Foundation kicks up a lot of adverse publicity?"

He grinned. "Especially."

A short time later Frannie, who had been under full sail supervising the caterer's crew, hove to at the booth. "Oh, Emma! You've got to give me one of those leaflets."

I handed her one from the nearest stack. She began fanning herself. "Gracious! I had no idea it would be so warm today. But isn't everything else turning out just wonderfully!"

"It certainly is." I was about to remark on how much all this had cost, but Jimmy, equipped with a hand microphone, began hallooing at the crowd and waving his straw hat for attention.

He welcomed everybody, then made short pitches for the Buckeye Foundation and the gold country hurrah. "If you want to know more," he said, "there's plenty of literature over there in the booth. Meanwhile, we're all here to have a good time."

That brought cheers.

Jimmy went on, introducing both Amos and Hiram and explaining the afternoon's schedule. "And, for all the delicious food and drink we have here this afternoon, let's all give a big round of Buckeye applause for Mrs. Frannie Edmundson."

Frannie blushed prettily. Then, as a scattering of applause began, waved her beribboned hat.

"That's right, folks, there she is, over by the Buckeye Foundation tent—Mrs. Frannie Edmundson, social director of the Buckeye Foundation!"

This time the applause was considerable. Frannie, still blushing, waved again in acknowledgment.

"Frannie," I said when the commotion had died down, "how on earth did you get enough money for all this?"

"Oh . . ." She gave a little shrug. "I just found some ways to do things. It doesn't take much to make a big impression." She waved airily. "A few potted plants, some balloons . . ."

The words were innocent, but not Frannie's expression.

"Frannie . . ." I used my severest tones.

She glanced at the caterer's tent, at Hiram's car, then over at Amos's displays. Finally, her gaze came to rest somewhere near my shirt pocket. "It doesn't take so much," she repeated doggedly. She looked up at me and put on a smile. "Don't you remember what Trooper said?" she asked brightly. She gave a credible imitation of Trooper's Mae West shoulder wiggle. "It's the perception that counts."

I remained silent.

"Trooper would have liked the party, don't you think?"

Our conversation was interrupted by a loud but melodic toot. Coming up the hill was a flatbed truck, brightly painted. On the back was a steam calliope. There were two more toots. Wisps of steam wafted on the breeze.

"Ladies and gentlemen!" Jimmy called out, circus ring-master style. "May I present the extra added attraction of the afternoon, Gillespie's world-famous superdeluxe steam calliope, Nelson DeWitt at the keyboard. Yessir! We'll have music this afternoon, courtesy of generous donations to the Buckeye Foundation."

The crowd applauded wildly. Nelson DeWitt gave a shave and a haircut, two bits salute. The truck continued up the hill.

"Frannie!" I fixed her with my best gimlet eye. "Where did the money come from?"

Frannie again gave careful study to the Buckeye Foundation tent, Hiram's car, my shirt pocket. "Oh, you aren't the only sleuth around here."

"What's that supposed to mean?"

"Well, nobody else was checking into it, so I did."

"Checked into *what?*"

She looked at me at last. "When we were talking about the graves of those poor Chinese workmen, Amos said there was another place, too, but the land had been dredged."

I remembered. But I'd seen it as an atrocity long since over and done with—too late to mend.

"That was terrible!" Frannie said. "Just terrible!" She shook her head in disapproval. "Well, I got to talking to people to learn who was in charge back then—of the dredging, I mean."

I was beginning to put two and two together.

"It was Mr. McCready," Frannie said, her indignation clear. "He was new, just assigned to his post. But that's no excuse. He let it happen."

"Frannie, you didn't—"

"I most certainly did! I asked myself what the best restitution was that we could get, and it was to further the cause of preserving the Chinese places here. So I marched right over to Mr. McCready's office and—"

The calliope truck arrived at the parking lot and burst into a rousing rendition of "When the Saints Come Marching

In." I had to shout to make myself heard. "You hit McCready up for this party?"

She nodded, a mischievous gleam in her eye. "I was helping," she yelled, at the same time pointing to the Buckeye Foundation tent. "The right image." She did the shoulder wiggle business again, then mouthed the Mae West words. "It's the perception that counts."

Trooper would have loved it.